Honey Homicide

A
Backyard Farming
Mystery

BOOK 3

VIKKI WALTON

Morewellson, Ltd.

Morewellson, L.T.D.
PO Box 49726
Colorado Springs, Colorado 80949

ISBN **978-0-9994402-3-0** (standard edition print)

Front Cover Illustration: Erica Parker Rogers
Formatting by Rik-Wild Seas Formatting
WildSeasFormatting.com

Primary Cast of Characters

Anne Fremont: Even though she's now settled in Carolan Springs, trouble keeps knocking on her door.

Bill and Lori Connor: Beekeeper Bill Connor is caring for his ill wife, Lori, but how far will he go to help her?

Sheriff Carson: As Lori's cousin, Carson fears Lori's illness may have caused Bill to get involved in something dangerous.

Deputy Benjamin Ruiz: Carson's deputy, whose actions betray his words.

Mary Smith: A visitor to Carolan Springs who Anne suspects may be something more than she lets on.

Police Chief Bradley Everett: The town's police chief who warns Anne about helping Carson.

Police Officer Dale: First on the scene after someone attacks Bill. Does he know more than he's saying?

…along with the residents of Carolan Springs: Hope, Kandi, Stewart, Spencer, Sam, and all the rest.

"Something was jigging and worrying in his brain; it felt like a hive of bees, stirred up by a stick." Dorothy L. Sayers (Whose Body)

Chapter One

Anne panicked.

Nowhere to run.

She backed up as far as she could, but her pursuer came closer.

Closer.

Fear gripped her.

"Don't swat at it," a male voice spoke firmly.

Anne heard the admonition at the exact moment her hand had risen toward her face.

Bill, the beekeeper giving the presentation, walked over to her. Anne became aware of many white-veiled heads turning toward her.

She lowered her arm as the bee continued to buzz close to her head. It was hard not to wave it away. Bill grinned and patted her on the arm.

"Not to worry, young lady. Being around bees the first time can be a bit scary for some. But trust me, they don't want to sting you." He held out his ungloved hand in front of him.

Anne backed up, and the bee stopped buzzing around her face. The bee landed on Bill's hand and began sucking at droplets of honey that remained from when he'd pulled off a chunk of honeycomb for the others to see.

"Aren't you afraid of getting stung?" Anne took a step closer to where the bee continued to focus on the honey.

"No. I'm not saying you shouldn't be cautious, but I've been stung many times over the years. It's usually when I haven't been listening to the girls."

"Listening? What do you mean?" Anne laughed. "Do they say, 'hey, leave us alone or we'll sting you?'"

"Something like that. You can actually tell how the bees are feeling by listening to the hive. Different times of the day make a difference on how they react. Lots of reasons. So yes, I do listen to them."

The bee, now sated, flew up from his hand and moved back toward Anne.

Bill's brow crinkled. He moved closer to Anne and sniffed. "Is that lemongrass I smell?"

"Um, yes." Anne nodded. "Why?"

Bill laughed boisterously. "Didn't you get the message on fragrance? Bees love lemongrass. In fact, we often add a drop of lemongrass oil into a container if we're trying to catch a swarm."

"I thought that you said no perfume. I didn't realize that meant oils too." Her face flamed with embarrassment. Of course, if she could smell it, so could others. Even bees.

"It's fine. But that's why you had that bee so intent on coming after you. It doesn't have to be perfume. It's any type of fragrance these bees think are flowers. They spend their days searching for nectar and pollen."

"I may not be cut out to be a beekeeper. That was just one bee. I saw you pick up that frame with all those bees all over it and flying around and I had to get away. It's really scary."

Bill took Anne by the arm and nodded to the other beekeepers to continue the class. He walked away with her until they were farther from the group and could see his house.

"Let's get you calm and then we'll go back and join the class. Once you start learning about bees, you'll lose that fear. But for now, take a break and get your bearings."

As they ambled away from the group Anne could still hear Bill's assistant discussing the types of bees—Carolian, Italian, Russian. It sounded like a talk on global issues.

The pair walked on a bit and Bill paused. He turned toward his house. In the window, Anne could see a woman silhouetted in the frame. The frail woman sat in a large overstuffed chair and had a blanket over her lap. A bright scarf covered where her beautiful raven hair used to be. The woman looked up from her book and waved at the pair.

Anne smiled and waved back.

Bill nodded toward the house. "You want to see something really scary? Cancer, that's what's really scary. It's even worse when you have no control and you can't do anything about it." He waved at the house and his wife blew him a kiss.

"I'm really sorry, Bill. I know it has to be hard on you."

They started walking back to the group. "Nothing like it is on Lori. She never complains. I know she's in pain, but she tries to stay positive."

"Bill, if there's anything I can do… Please, I'd like to help."

"Not much anyone can do. It's in God's hands now, but we're doing what we can. And the … um, never mind, but we're trying something new and it seems to be helping manage the pain."

"Well, that's good."

He sighed. "Yes, that's one of the good things."

"What? I can tell you're troubled about something?"

"No. Well, yes. I'm just stressed out. To be perfectly honest, our bills have been mounting for the last few months and I just don't know how we'll be able to continue to pay for Lori's treatments." He sighed and shook his head. "I'm sorry. I don't know why I shared that. We don't even know each other that well."

"It's okay. I'm sure that you have a huge burden on your shoulders, and you can feel okay in talking to me. I won't say anything to anyone."

"Thanks."

"Have you ever thought of doing a fundraiser? I'm sure people here in the Springs would be happy to help you both."

"No." He faltered. "I've been offered an, um, opportunity to make some money, and I'm thinking I may take it."

"Why do I sense some hesitation?"

"It's not really…never mind. I haven't decided yet. It's something I could have never seen me being involved with in a million years. But I'd do anything to make sure Lori is cared for and doesn't suffer."

Anne glanced over at Bill. What could Bill be thinking of doing that could be causing him so much angst?

"Well, if it could help Lori and bring in some more money too, then it sounds like something to consider."

"Yes. That's what I'm doing. Not rushing into it. Just considering it."

"That's great to hear. But, seriously," she laid her hand on his arm. "I'm here to help. Please know that."

"Thank you." He patted her gloved hand.

They'd arrived back to where the frames had been returned to the Langstroth hives. Bill's assistant was putting on the top cover and while some bees were buzzing around, there weren't as many. The group moved away from the hive and started pulling off veils, white jackets, overalls and gloves.

Kandi removed her veil and sprinted over to Anne. "Wasn't that, *like*, the coolest thing ever?"

"Maybe the scariest." Anne removed her veiled helmet. "Weren't you afraid of being stung?"

Kandi shook her head, her long earrings dancing about her neck. "Nope. After Nate said that only half could sting you, that made a big difference."

"Only half?" Anne queried. "What do you mean?"

Kandi giggled. "Oh, that must have been when you were trying to outrun that bee."

"Ha Ha." Anne stuffed her gloves inside the hat. "Go on." Anne walked beside the young woman, who was smoothing down her hair after removing her hat and veil.

"Well, there's the workers—that's the girls, and then there's the drones—the boys. They can't sting you."

"Oh, I didn't know that. I thought they could all sting you." Anne looked over to where a group of people were talking. The group was staying at the Brandywine Inn, which was owned by Anne, Kandi, and Hope, who also ran the local herbal shop. The group would be returning to the Inn shortly.

"I know. I learned a lot today. I'm glad we're thinking of getting some hives for the Inn but I'm thinking we should consider a top bar versus the Langstroth."

"Huh?" Anne quipped.

"It's the different types of hives. Nate said we might want to think about them."

"Okay, well, we can get with Hope and discuss it." She cocked her head to the group. "Right now, I think we need to get with our guests and see if they'll be returning to the Inn or going into town for lunch."

"Sounds good." Kandi fell in beside Anne. The group had walked over to a driveway where cars had trunks open and gear was being collected. "I saw you talking with Bill. How's Lori doing?"

"I think she's doing as good as can be expected. Hard to say when you've basically been handed a death sentence."

"It's sad." A tear slipped down Kandi's cheek. "She's always been so nice to me."

"Ahh, honey." Anne put her arm around the young woman. "You're so tender-hearted and sweet."

"Of course, I'm sweet—you just called me honey." Kandi laughed as she wiped her cheek.

"You goof." Anne squeezed the woman in a quick hug.

They'd arrived at the car when Kandi's phone went off.

"Hi, Hope. What's up?" She listened and her face paled. "She's right here. Hold on."

Kandi handed the phone to Anne. "Hi, Hope. What's up?"

"The Bennett's place caught on fire and they need a place to stay. I was going to offer them a place at the Inn at no charge but wanted to check with you all first."

"Certainly." Anne put the phone on speaker, so Kandi could also hear Hope too. Kandi drew closer to the phone. "Did it destroy their home, *like*, completely?"

Hope's voice carried, "No. Only part of it. But it's damaged badly enough that they can't stay there. But it did destroy their greenhouse." A moment of silence passed.

"Hope, what else?"

"You know me too well, Anne. They found a body in the greenhouse."

Chapter Two

"We're in here." Anne heard Hope call out from the kitchen.

Anne walked into the room.

Faith, Hope's mother, sat at the table. She looked up from her cup as the pair came into the room. A woman appeared from the back office.

"Eliza!"

"Anne." The pair embraced.

"When did you get back into town?" Anne pulled out a chair and Hope held up a cup. Anne nodded assent.

"I arrived last night and thought I would stop by this morning. I hope that you will excuse my appearance."

"Only if you'll excuse mine." Anne winked.

Anne and Eliza were as different as night and day in their looks and their outfits. Anne was a medium height with a new layered haircut and a touch of blond highlights. Her preferred clothing was anything clean and comfortable. In contrast, Eliza was a tall, graceful woman that had come from Ethiopia. Eliza was a hand model who traveled globally on assignments. She was always impeccably dressed, and her hair was now piled atop her head in braids. A bright scarf wound around her forehead keeping the braids secure. She wore a running outfit but even it looked like something from the runway.

As Anne and Eliza received a cup of tea from Hope, Kandi pranced into the room. "Eliza!" She hugged the woman who smiled widely.

"Hello, Kandi. It is so good to see you."

Kandi also embraced Faith. "Hiya, Miss Faith. I'm so glad you came over with Hope for a visit."

"I like visiting Ralph's house. It's so nice that he lets you stay here." Faith smiled.

A glance passed between Hope and Kandi. Some days were better than others with Faith's memory.

Hope bent down by her mother. "Mama, do you remember that this is now the Brandywine Inn? Kandi, Anne and I have made it into a bed and breakfast."

Faith patted Hope's hand. "That's nice. Ralph always liked Brandywine tomatoes."

"Yes, he did. In fact—" Hope rose. "We're growing some out in the garden. Do you want to go see them?"

She helped Faith to her feet, and the pair went outside.

"She's so good to her mother." Eliza took a sip of her tea. "I heard that you all had things happen since I've been away."

Kandi plopped down on a chair. She pulled a scrunchy off her wrist, pulled her bright red hair into a pile and using the scrunchy made a top knot. "Our opening weekend was a doozy—"

"You can say that again." Anne set her cup on the table.

"Our opening…"

"Funny. You goof." Anne swatted at Kandi.

"But things are better now?" Eliza's tone was serious.

"Yes, much better. The guests we have this time are actually normal." Anne knocked on the wood table with her knuckles.

"You were over at Bill's today learning about bees?"

"Yes." Anne got up. "Here, I brought back some of his honey. I know you like to put honey in your hand creams."

"Thank you. That's very thoughtful of you."

"We like to provide a goodie basket when the guests arrive, so we're thinking of adding honey. Then we can have a Brandywine Inn tea and honey for the guests."

Just then the back door swung open. A young, lanky teenager appeared. He wore a red tee-shirt and a pair of holey blue jeans. He pulled off his cap. "I finished the mowing, Ms. Freemont. I dumped all the clippings over in the compost pile in your yard as you said. Anything else you need from me today?"

"I think that's all. Did you take Bear for a walk yet?"

Eliza's eyebrows shot up.

Anne turned to her. "I'll explain later."

"I planned on doing that now. I figured I'd take him over to Patty's as we need to get more dog food."

"Geez. That dog eats a lot." Anne took a sip of her tea.

Spencer went to the sink and washed his hands. He turned back to Anne and waited.

Anne sighed. "Okay, tell Patty to put it on my card."

Spencer nodded. He turned to Eliza. "I'm sorry. I should have introduced myself. I'm Spencer Andrews. I'm their helper."

Eliza shook Spencer's extended hand. "Nice to meet you, Spencer. You can call me Eliza."

"Nice to meet you, Ms. Eliza." The boy put his cap back on his head and walked out the back door. They heard him call out, "Bear!"

Anne got up from her seat and washed her cup. She put it on the drainer beside the sink.

"I best depart as well." Eliza rose, and Anne took her cup from her.

"How about dinner this week? Would that work for you? We could go to that new place in town or wherever you'd like?" Anne washed Eliza's cup.

"That sounds nice. I'd love to do that. Unfortunately, I'm home for a short time before I have to leave for another shoot. I only have the next few days."

Hope had returned with Faith, who she sat in a rocking chair. "What are you all planning?"

"I said we should get together for dinner. You in?"

"That sounds good. Is it okay if we swing by Bill and Lori's afterward? I have some things to drop off to them."

Stewart had come in while the group was talking. "Did you hear about that fire up close at the Bennett's place?"

"Yes. It's horrible. We offered to let them stay here but they decided to go into Denver." Hope put a cup in the dishwasher.

Stewart leaned up against the counter. "Their greenhouse and barn are completely destroyed. The house has some damage, but it's salvageable. They weren't home when it happened."

"Oh no. That's horrible. How are they faring?"

Stewart ran his hands through his brown hair. He shoved the sleeves of his flannel shirt up.

"You know. It's strange. But usually when a fire happens, people have all kinds of emotions, but it was different with Cam."

"What do you mean? Was he angry or…?"

"No. Nothing like that. It was fear."

Later the talk turned to food and they all decided to go out for dinner that evening.

Eliza sat in the front as Hope drove over to the restaurant, while Anne and Kandi sat in the back.

"I like your new car, Hope," Eliza commented.

"Thanks. I figured I should get something better suited to our Colorado weather."

Kandi joined in. "I still say you should have gotten a truck or an SUV instead of this Subaru but up to you."

"Thanks, Mom." Hope laughed. "This works for me. I don't plan on going out into the backcountry."

The group chatted amiably as they headed to the Connor's house.

They arrived at the front door and rang the bell.

No answer.

"Hmmm, that's strange. I called earlier and said we'd be dropping by. Lori said this would be a good time."

Anne rang the bell again.

"Was Bill going out? Maybe it's taking Lori some time to get to the door. She is really frail." Hope answered back.

Kandi cocked her head. "Do you all hear something?"

"What do you mean?"

The group stopped and listened.

"I hear something." Hope walked around toward the back of the house. The rest of the ladies followed.

They could hear a faint cry.

"I think it's coming from, *like*, over there." Kandi pointed.

Anne and Hope turned toward the greenhouse.

"Help. Please. Help me!" It was Lori.

Had she fallen?

Kandi rushed over to where Lori lay on the ground. "Are you okay?"

Lori pointed toward the greenhouse. "Please. Go."

Hope stayed with Lori while the others made their way to the greenhouse. Inside, it looked like a tornado had gone through it. Pots were broken on the flagstone path and plants pulled up, but what quickly caught Anne's attention was Bill. He lay slumped on the floor, a big gash on his head.

"Kandi, call 911." Kandi reached into her pocket and grabbed her cellphone. As she spoke, Anne rushed over to the man and knelt down beside him.

"Bill. Bill. Can you hear me?" Anne knew it was best not to move someone with a head injury.

"Is he dead?" Eliza grasped her long fingers around her neck.

"No. But it doesn't look good. He's got a nasty looking cut on his head."

"Here." Eliza pulled a clean monogramed handkerchief from her pocket. She handed it to Anne.

Anne wiped the blood from Bill's face. It appeared that the cut to his head was his only injury. Had he fallen and hit his head? But what about all the damage? Bill groaned. He moved to raise his hand to his head.

"Don't move, Bill. You've been hurt. Help is on the way." Anne looked up as Kandi came in the door.

"The ambulance is on the way. Like what happened in here?" Kandi face grimaced as she looked around. "Bill, *like*, loves this greenhouse."

"Let's talk about that later," Anne admonished. "Sweetie, can you run up to the house and see if they have a blanket we can use?"

Bill groaned again. He gathered his breath, then whispered, "Attacked."

Chapter Three

They were silent as the EMS team loaded Bill onto the gurney. After Bill went off in the ambulance, the women watched as Police Chief Bradley Everett spoke with Sam. He nodded his head and then strode over to meet the women. "Ladies. I hear that you were the ones to find Mr. Connor."

Anne spoke first. "We were on our way over as Hope had a few items she wanted to give Lori."

"Poor Lori. First, her cancer and now this." Everett pulled his hat off and stuck it under his arm. His hair was an indeterminate color because of the closely shaved buzz cut. He wiped his head and then put the hat back on. Pulling out a notepad, he clicked his pen. "Now then, you were here when the event happened?"

"Oh, no," Hope responded. "We were at the front door. We rang the doorbell, but no one answered."

"What happened then?"

We heard someone calling for help. He looked up from his notes. "Was that Bill?"

"No, it was Lori Connor," Hope replied. "We went around the back and there she was on the ground. I think she'd tried to go to the greenhouse, but it's too far from the house for her. She had collapsed."

"She saw nothing?" Everett spoke to Hope.

"Like what?" Anne clasped her hands together.

"From the preliminary review, it looks like Bill may have caught some vandals in his greenhouse."

"So, he was, *like,* attacked?" Kandi shivered. "Oh, how awful."

Why would someone destroy a greenhouse? It made no sense. Plus, Bill and Lori's house isn't on the main road or anything.

Anne started to say her questions out loud then decided against it.

"Did you all notice any teenagers or anyone leaving the area?"

"No," the group replied in unison.

"Why?" Anne rubbed her arms and looked toward the greenhouse. Something just didn't add up. Why attack Bill so savagely?

Another police officer had joined the group. The officer spoke. His eyes were shielded from view by his large, dark aviator sunglasses. He nodded toward the greenhouse. "We've been having a lot of vandalism around town lately. Even quite a few fires being set."

"Oh, that's horrible," Eliza spoke up. "You believe that it is a bunch of hoodlums?"

Anne pursed her lips together. Only Eliza would choose the word hoodlums.

"We believe so." He nodded toward the greenhouse. "So, just to confirm." He looked at his notes. "You arrived, and Lori Connor was on the ground. Was she able to tell you anything she saw or heard? It could be helpful."

Hope answered. "No. I stayed with her. She said she'd been in the house, waiting on us when she heard some noise. She wasn't sure what it was, so she went to the window. She couldn't see Bill, so she became worried. When she tried to walk out to the greenhouse, it was too much for her. That's when we found her."

"She didn't see a person or hear a car?"

Hope shook her head. "No, she was just worried about Bill, as she had called him on his cell, and he hadn't answered."

Chief Everett nodded. "Then you all went to the greenhouse. Can you tell me your steps?"

Anne replied, "When we reached the door, I saw that Bill was injured so I told Kandi to call 911. She went outside the greenhouse. Eliza and I saw that Bill had been hurt."

"Did he say anything to you?" He cocked his head.

"He only said one word, 'attacked' but he wasn't fully conscious." Anne rubbed her upper arms.

"It certainly looks like someone attacked him. But we must do more investigation." He pointed toward a broken area of the greenhouse. "I'm guessing whoever did this entered and exited that way and then ran into the cover of the woods."

But why? That was the question that kept coming up in Anne's mind.

Chapter Four

The EMS team had taken Lori to the hospital as well. As soon as Everett had finished his questions, the group returned to their vehicle.

"I feel so sorry for Bill and Lori. Like they just keep having bad things happen to them," Kandi noted.

"Unfortunately, that's life sometimes." Hope steered the car back to town. Eliza bid the group a good evening and headed home to pack for her trip.

Kandi shook her head and spoke aloud. "Why would someone want to destroy the greenhouse though? It makes no sense."

"Maybe just because they can. Vandals don't care." Anne interjected.

The trio drove over to the Inn. "I'll check on the guests and then I will call it a night," Hope replied. She gave Kandi a hug as the young woman turned toward her house.

Kandi screamed.

What had happened? A knot formed in Anne's throat.

Kandi jumped up and down and ran toward her house. On the front steps were two young men. While taller than Kandi, their appearance made it clear that these were Kandi's twin brothers that Anne had never met. They moved toward Kandi, who ran into their arms.

Anne and Hope walked over to the group. The boys had pulled Kandi up into a hug, three red heads pushed together. They were all smiling and laughing. Finally, they set her down on the ground.

Kandi pulled Anne over toward them. "This is Anne. Mom. I've told you all about her." Anne shook one hand and then the other. "Nice to meet you in person."

"Likewise. I'm Karl." He grinned widely beneath a tuft of a mustache.

"I'm Kevin." Unlike Karl, Kevin had a full beard.

Both looked like they had spent plenty of time outdoors. Their faces were weathered, and they wore their hair long. Kevin had pulled his hair back in a ponytail while Karl's just hung limply around his face.

"Why didn't you call me?" Kandi playfully punched at the pair. "When did you get in?"

"How about we go inside?" Anne replied as Hope waved but headed back toward the Inn.

Karl crouched down and grabbed a grungy duffel bag while Kevin hiked a khaki backpack over his shoulder.

Kandi opened the door and led them back toward the kitchen. "I can take you up to your rooms in a minute, unless you need or want to go up now."

"I'm good." Karl stretched and bent over into a yoga pose. "That plane ride was the worst."

Anne said, "I think Kandi had told me you all were hiking in—Nepal, was it?"

"Yes, that was the last place we visited. We would have come home sooner when things happened with Kandi—"

"Ugh, don't remind me." Kandi looked at Anne who recalled when Kandi had been accused of a horrible crime.

"Kandi, I'm going to see if Hope needs help to prepare for when the guests come back to the Inn. That way, you all can catch up a bit more." She smiled at them. "How about coming over for dinner this evening?"

"Sounds good to me," Kevin replied. "I'm a vegan and Karl is vegetarian so not sure if that makes a difference."

Anne hugged Kandi. "Okay, see you later." Anne took the shortcut between Kandi's and the Brandywine Inn's backyard. The guests hadn't returned yet, so Anne and Hope set up a tray of brownies and popcorn in the living area. They restocked the little fridge with waters, juices, and sodas.

"I think we're good for when they return. Now, an important question." Anne looked intently at Hope.

"What's that? You look awfully serious."

"What can I cook that a vegan and a vegetarian would eat?"

Hope laughed. "Not to worry. I can handle it."

The guests returned to the Inn and were settled into the living room with snacks and drinks.

"I'm off." Anne closed the file she'd been working on and shut down the computer.

Hope looked up from a book she'd been reading about bees. "I think I'll head out too. Kandi was going to take the next shift. Should I come back?"

"No need. I can do that. I'll just pop home for a bit and then come back."

The back door banged open. Stewart saw the women and hurried over to them.

"What is it, Stewart? You look like you've seen a ghost." Hope motioned to a chair, but Stewart shook his head to the negative.

"I just… I can't believe it." He ran his hand over his face.

Anne reached over and took hold of his arm. "Stewart. Please. We can tell you're shook up. Sit down and you can tell us what happened."

He slumped into the chair that Hope had just abandoned. His elbows on his knees, he covered his face with his hands and took in deep breaths.

Anne and Hope made eyes at each other. They'd never known Stewart to lose his composure. He finally looked up.

"I guess I shouldn't be surprised. But it's always a shock. No matter what."

The women waited.

"It's Ray. We went to high school together. We were friends. Really good friends. Then he got in with the wrong crowd."

He looked at Anne and Hope's questioning faces. "Drugs."

They nodded.

"His dad had been hurt in a serious car accident and was on lots of painkillers. Ray got access to them and then started selling them." He shook his head. "Not surprisingly, he got caught. They sent him to 'juvey' and we lost touch. I'd seen him a few months back. He'd come back to town, but he was so different. I guess that's what drugs do to you. Hardens you."

Anne leaned on the desk. "Sorry to hear that you and Ray are no longer friends. It does happen."

Stewart shook his head vehemently. "No. No. That's not it." He rubbed his hands together. "The Bennett's place. It was Ray. They found Ray."

"I'm sorry." Hope responded. "I think we're missing something. I know the Bennetts had a fire at their place."

Stewart looked at them. "That's just it. The body they found in the greenhouse rubble when they were searching after the fire. It was Ray's."

Chapter Five

Anne left Hope in charge of figuring out the menu for the evening. She returned to her house to check on Mouser and to set up the food and treat trays for when she'd be next door at the Inn.

Hope had finally persuaded Stewart to go over to Kandi's. Anne had waved to the pair as they walked over to Kandi's.

Got to hand it to her. She's a shrewd woman. Hope knows that Kandi will be the balm for Stewart's sorrow.

As Anne pulled back the tab on the can of salmon, a meow caught her attention. Mouser, ever aloof when it suited him, rubbed up against her legs. She picked him up and he purred loudly.

"Don't even think about it. I know you're just trying to get me to give you a treat early."

He meowed.

"Okay. Fine. Just a couple." Anne picked up a couple of the treats from the open box and Mouser ate them. After he had licked her fingers, she set him down.

She closed the boxes and set the timers. "Okay, then I'm off." She pointed to Mouser. "No wild parties while I'm gone." His black fuzzy tail swished back and forth.

Anne wondered what he was thinking. Probably something along the lines of "You are my servant."

Anne turned the light on over the kitchen sink and the light in the hallway, so that later on she wouldn't come home to a dark house. Even as an adult, she preferred coming into a home with lights on which chased away any scary shadows.

The sun was still shining brightly in the sky even though it was late in the afternoon. Hope had called and said that Autumn, who was also a vegan, had decided to cook up a lentil curry for the evening meal. With a large salad and some naan bread, they were set, so Anne was off the hook for preparing any dinner tonight.

Anne opened the door and heard laughter coming from the dining room. She smiled. This was so much better than all the arguing that had been part and parcel of the Inn's first set of guests. She walked into the dining room where four ladies sat playing Apples to Apples.

"All well here?"

"Yes," replied Mrs. Adams. She and her husband had been guests at the Inn for the last few days and had attended the lecture on bees and hives. "We've really enjoyed our stay here. I've already told Mike I want to reserve our room now for the homesteading fair this fall, before you get booked up."

"That's wonderful." Anne picked up empty cups on the sideboard. "Let me know tomorrow when you leave, and I'll get the room reserved."

"Will you have the upstairs suite done by then?" Another guest raised her head. "My husband couldn't come this time as he was working, and I'd like to bring the kids too. I think that could work for us."

Anne, Hope, and Kandi had decided to turn the attic into a large suite with a bathroom that could serve as a room for four friends or a small family. Two beds were easily converted into a king-size bed and two other daybeds provided seating and sleeping arrangements. In addition, a small kitchenette with an apartment-size refrigerator, a microwave, and hot pot had already seen a lot of inquiries for reservations on their website.

After they'd cleared out the attic, they were amazed at how much more space they had. They'd included a table and four chairs for playing games. Like the other rooms in the Inn, it held no television only an area packed with various games and books for kids and adults. If people wanted to bring their own online entertainment, that was up to them, but the message of the Brandywine Inn was clear. Spend time off-line, outdoors, and with your family.

Anne realized she'd not answered but had been distracted by her thoughts. "Oh, I apologize. Yes, the room should be completed before the fair. I'd be happy to see if we have space for your family on the dates you want."

She nodded to the two other women and took the gathered cups to the kitchen for washing. She was humming to herself when the back door opened, and Spencer popped in. "

"Hey," he quipped.

"Hay is for horses." Anne set the wet cup on the drainer.

"What?"

"Never mind."

"Hope wanted me to add another calendar to the website about the attic room."

"Okay. I'm not using the computer, so this is as good a time as any."

Spencer didn't move. After spending time with him over the last few months, she'd begun to read this trait as him wanting to say something.

"What is it?"

He mumbled something.

"What? I can't understand you."

"Is it true that they found Ray Lawrence … his body … in the fire at the Bennetts?"

Anne laid down the dishcloth and faced Spencer. "Yes. Why?" She pointed for him to sit down. "Did you know him?"

Spencer sat on the edge of his chair. He shook his head. "No. I didn't know him. Well, I guess, I sort of knew him. But not really. But I did, you know, know of him."

Anne waited.

"I, well, he, um, I—"

"Spit it out. What is it?"

"I feel bad, but I'm not really sorry, he, you know, is dead."

"Spencer. Why would you…"

He bowed his head. "He wasn't a nice person."

"There are a lot of people who aren't nice people, but you don't wish them dead."

He started. "Oh, no. I didn't wish him dead. I, you know, just wanted him gone."

"Look, I know you're holding something back. Tell me."

"Well, you know that he was related to Ms. Lawrence, my foster mom?"

Anne nodded yes.

"But what you didn't know is that he was always selling pot to the other kids."

"What!"

"Oh, Mrs. Lawrence didn't know. She thought he was coming over because he wanted to stop kids from going the direction he had gone in school. But he was either selling them drugs or getting them to sell pot for him."

"That's horrible. Have you told anyone about this?"

"No way." Spencer looked at her with pleading eyes.

"I won't say anything. Don't worry. But only because he's dead."

Spencer let out a sigh.

"I appreciate your telling me everything." She nodded toward the office. "You probably should get to the computer work."

After Spencer had left, Anne sat at the table.

Ray Lawrence had been selling pot to the foster kids in Mrs. Lawrence care behind her back. But what was he doing over at the Bennett's place? All Anne knew was that the Bennetts were a young couple who'd moved into Carolan Springs last fall. She'd seen them only a few times. First, when they were welcomed into the community and a few times on Main Street.

Had Ray gone over to their house to sell them pot? With Colorado making marijuana legal, it wasn't a crime. At least for adults. But Ray had been selling to minors. That was a different story. Carolan Springs council had rejected the retail side of it but approved the medicinal shops. This had caused a lot of angst in their normally quiet company, with both sides fighting for what they thought was right.

She stood up and pushed the chair back under the table. She'd take a look around and then head over to Kandi's for dinner. She pulled out a tote that held various supplies along with bagged cookies and chocolates for the guests. Climbing the back stairs, Anne was happy to see Stewart had completed the addition of more lights to the ceiling. They'd also painted the walls a bright white, so the stairway had been transformed into something light and bright, versus dark and scary. As she made her way up the stairs, Anne thought to herself, *what stories these stairs could tell.*

After going through the rooms and making sure that the guests had chocolates on their pillows and their tea caddy full, along with a bag of shortbread cookies nearby, she headed back downstairs. Peeking into the office, she saw Spencer had already left. She closed the door and locked it. Time to head over to Kandi's.

Outside, a sheriff's cruiser drew up to the cul-de-sac's curb. It stopped, and Anne walked up to it.

The window on the passenger slid down.

Anne bent down to see the driver. "Deputy Ruiz. What are you doing over here? Nothing's happened I hope."

He pulled off his sunglasses. His skin had become a handsome shade of toffee brown, no doubt from time spent outside in the sun. Anne had heard he was a keen fisherman and would hike up into the backcountry for miles to a secluded mountain lake. If only she could tan so nicely. Anne sighed. While peaches and cream were nice, her skin only turned to a lobster shade with too much sun.

"No. But Sheriff Carson has us doing more sweeps of the area. We've been hearing about quite a few fires and we want to make sure we don't have an arsonist on our hands."

Nothing could cause more concern and fear than fire when it came to living in the mountains. A simple campfire could easily grow to destroy thousands of acres of land, kill wildlife and obliterate habitats, along with the destruction of homes and businesses. Someone who set fires intentionally had to be caught quickly.

"I heard about the Bennett's place. That was horrible."

"Yes. It's not confirmed but it looks like arson because of—"

"Ray Lawrence."

"How did you know about that?" He wiped his sunglasses and propped them on his head.

Anne shrugged. "Small town."

"I guess."

"Oh, before you go. I know that it's under the police's purview, but any word on the attack on Bill Connor?"

"No. That was a nasty business. He's still in the hospital with a concussion. I hate to see something like that happening here. It's why I got away from the city. I couldn't stop much there but I'm determined I will keep this town—" Ruiz stopped as Anne realized he'd begun talking more to himself than to her. He clamped his lips tightly together.

"Well, I know you're busy and I've got to get over to Kandi's."

"Did I see her brothers are back in town?"

"Yes. They arrived earlier today."

Anne saw him place his sunglasses back over his eyes. Did he not want her to see something?

"Okay. Well, better get going." He waved, and she backed away from the car. She saw the window go up as he made a slow pass on the road and then turned out of sight.

It sure seemed weird that he would be patrolling the area. As far as she knew, she'd never known the sheriff's department or the police to do neighborhood drive-bys.

Plus, how did he know about Kandi's brothers? Was he keeping tabs on everyone? She didn't know whether to think this was a good thing or a foreboding of bad things to come.

Chapter Six

After a delicious supper, the group all moved out to Kandi's deck.

"That was a wonderful dinner, Autumn. I didn't think I'd like lentil curry as much as I did," Anne complimented the young woman.

Kevin had moved over closer to Autumn. Karl hung back, but it was blatantly obvious that he was infatuated with the young woman as well.

Anne recounted the conversation she'd had with Spencer to Hope.

Kevin broke into the conversation. "They falsely accuse marijuana as a gateway drug. There are other things more harmful."

Hope interjected before Anne could respond, "Yes, it can be considered an herb, which has therapeutic value, but it can also have contraindications as many herbs do. It's certainly not a cure-all but I agree it doesn't deserve the venom—"

"Totally agree," Kevin responded.

"Conversely, it isn't a panacea for every ill and can be harmful like any drug." Hope took a sip of her drink.

Anne smothered a laugh. It was rare for Hope to take a strong position to other's statements.

Kandi said, "I hope, *like*, Spencer stays away from it."

"It's no worse than that drink you have in your hand." Karl nodded to the glass of wine Kandi held.

"That may be true. But kids need to stay away from any form of drug."

"Well said, Kandi." Anne nodded at the young woman.

"Thanks, Mom." Kandi smiled.

Karl and Kevin looked at one another. It was clear they didn't care for this new understanding between Kandi and Anne. Had Karl and Kevin felt differently about their mother's abandonment when they were younger?

"All I'm saying is that they should allow people to live their lives the way they choose," Kevin replied.

"I will agree with you on that, with one caveat," Hope responded. "Anything that someone chooses should not affect others. Taking drugs—of any source—rarely achieves that."

Anne could tell tempers were simmering under the surface. "You know what they say about politics and religion—that you shouldn't talk about them at dinner. Maybe this issue should be for a different time or conversation."

The group laughed, and even though Anne could tell that Hope and Karl wanted to continue the debate, they nodded agreement.

"On another note," Kandi interjected, "I received a call from Lori. She's staying in the hospital a few days and she said that Bill is still unconscious. It sounds like it's pretty touch-and-go with him."

"Sorry to hear that." Anne pushed her hair behind her ear. "I still wonder who would do such a thing."

"I will go over tomorrow and see about fixing the greenhouse. I know that if—I mean, when—Bill and Lori come home, I don't want it to remind them of the attack."

Anne nodded. "Good idea, Hope. I'll go with you."

"We can help too. We're not doing anything tomorrow." Kevin stood up.

"I'll be, *like,* busy with the breakfast at the Inn, but I can prepare a picnic lunch and bring it over," Kandi chirped.

"Sounds like a great plan." Hope stood and turned to Kandi. "Let's get things cleaned up so we can get out of your hair for the night."

"Go on Hope. Mom, can you help me?"

"Sure. Be happy to."

Hope turned to Autumn. "Ready to go?"

Autumn stood up. "Yes. Just let me get my Birks on and we can hit the trail."

"Trail?" Kevin cracked his knuckles.

Kandi placed stacked dishes on the counter. "Remember where we used to go down in the woods? In the last few years, while you guys have been traveling the world, they created a trail for walkers and runners."

"Just like the government to come in and destroy the environment to appease the people."

"Um, okay. Then don't go." Kandi threw up her hands.

"No. I want to go. I can walk over with you and then jog back. I need a run," he replied.

"Karl, do you want to join us?"

"Why not? It would be good to see the old area. We barely saw Main Street coming into town."

After the twins, Autumn, and Hope had said their goodbyes, Kandi turned to Anne. "Brothers!"

Chapter Seven

Anne and Hope drove over to Bill and Lori's house the next morning. After breakfast, Kandi would come over and her brothers said they would come too.

Anne parked her vehicle behind a dark green Focus. It was Lori's car. She hadn't driven herself home, but Anne hadn't remembered the car being there when they'd visited for the beehive workshop.

Hope opened her door and exited the car as a tall man walked from around the corner of the house.

It took a minute for Anne to realize it was Sheriff Carson. This was the first time she'd seen him out of his uniform. Today he wore a faded red pullover shirt, a pair of cargo pants and boat shoes sans socks. In place of his usual Stetson, he wore a black cap.

Seeing them, Carson removed his cap and his aviator sunglasses. He folded them and stuck them in the neck of his shirt. "Ladies. What are you doing here?"

"We wanted to come and clean up the greenhouse before Bill and Lori got home. Is it still a crime scene?"

"No. I wanted to look around myself. I checked on Lori—"

Anne interrupted him. "How is she doing? How's Bill? Will they get to come home soon? Any news on who did this? Anyone arrested?"

"Ahhh, ND. I see you haven't changed."

Anne had gotten used to his nickname for her from the initials of Nancy Drew. She'd turned down his offer to start up a relationship—no way was she going to be in something with him while he was still involved with Sorcha, the town's sultry bookstore owner. Ever since then, they'd been polite, and he usually called her Ms. Freemont. But he was out of uniform. Maybe that was it.

He continued. "Lori 's doing as well as can be expected after the shock. She will be coming home tomorrow so she asked if I could go to the repair shop and pick up her car for her."

"That's a strange thing for a sheriff to do, isn't it?" Anne pushed her hair back from her face.

"We're second cousins."

"Oh, I didn't know that."

"You know, there are a lot of things you don't know about me."

"Well…" Why had things become so uncomfortable all of a sudden?

Hope opened the back door and pulled out gloves and a hat. She handed a pair to Anne and stuck a pair under her arm. She also pulled out trash bags and some clippers. "Better get started. Nice seeing you, Sheriff Carson." She moved off toward the back.

Anne stood facing Carson. The silence stretched between them for a minute.

"Anne—"

She started. He rarely called her by her first name. She couldn't do this. Not now. "Good seeing you,

Sheriff Carson. We've got a lot of work to do. Bye." She sprinted off toward the back before he could respond.

As she moved out of his sight, she slowed to a walk, but her heart was pounding in her chest. *What's the matter with me? I'm not some young girl with a schoolgirl crush. I'm happy being on my own. I have my house, my work, Mouser. I don't need anything, or anyone, else.*

She stopped. If Carson brought the car here, how was he going to get back to town? She twisted to see him walking a bike onto the driveway. He turned and faced her, but his eyes were now obscured by his sunglasses and he'd put his cap back on. She waved, but he didn't return the gesture.

Hope called out, "Anne, can you give me a hand with this?"

Anne yelled, "Coming." When she turned back, Carson was peddling down the drive.

Arriving at the greenhouse, Anne noticed the smudges of fingerprints now visible because of the CSI technicians. She followed Hope into the space. The greenhouse was beautiful and larger than Anne would have thought. Along one wall were blue barrels for rainwater catchment. On the other side that faced east, someone had built planters at knee height in a large 'E' pattern, mimicking a traditional keyhole garden. The south side held a bunch of perennials and it surprised Anne to see a fig tree and a lemon plant.

Anne had heard they used climate-controlled greenhouses to grow various food and fruit in Basalt, but this was the first time she'd actually seen one.

"Oh wow. This is wonderful. I'm envious." Anne's face fell as she took in the overturned table and chairs along with the large broken pot. "Is that"—she pointed—"what they believe they hit him with?"

"Not sure. But look at this." Hope led Anne over to a door. Opening it they came into a small hallway. On either side of the hallway were storage rooms. One side held pots and various gardening tools. The other side was empty, apart from new shelving and a bunch of lights stacked in a corner.

"It looks like he's going to make this into a grow-room. I guess he feels he needs a more secure place for starting seedlings." Anne motioned to the main part of the greenhouse.

"Possibly." Hope waved with her hand. "Look at this." She walked past packed dirt walls that had been painted with what looked like a milk paint.

Hope opened the door, and they were standing outside again. Anne turned back toward where they'd exited for a better look. "Oh, that's really nice." She pointed to where the earth was full of wildflowers and clovers. Bees buzzed happily among the flowers and Anne noticed two skep hives closer to the top. She moved away from the back and shielded her eyes from the sun. Sure enough, a plastic tube connected the hive to the inside of the greenhouse.

"Well, that's smart. His bees can go inside the greenhouse too."

"Yes, but that's not why I brought you out here," Hope interjected. "I think the person who attacked Bill came in from this way. There's no lock on the door, and look—" She pointed to where the grass had been crushed. "I think someone was out here. Waiting."

She walked back inside. "They could have come in here and hidden in the potting shed. When they heard

Bill come in, they hit him with the pot." She inclined her head toward the broken pot.

"But wouldn't Bill have fought back?"

Hope waved toward the house. "Lori told me that Bill has a daily ritual. He comes down here and drinks tea inside the greenhouse." Hope went over and opened a small cabinet close to the table area. Inside were cups, saucers and tea tins. She reached down next to it and picked up an electric tea kettle.

"That could be true, but why do you think they were here in the first place?"

"That's what I wanted to show you." Hope moved over toward the raised beds. Under a pile of torn up tomatoes, she picked up a leaf and held it in front of Anne.

Anne gasped. "Marijuana. Whoa, I never saw that coming."

Chapter Eight

"It's not surprising. After all, with Lori's condition, pain management is the first consideration. People you never would have thought as 'pot-smokers' have seen its benefits."

"I guess. But I'm still not convinced. And isn't it illegal?" Anne looked to see if she could spot other plants among the foliage.

"No, it's not illegal here in Colorado. You can grow plants yourself. There's just a limit you can have growing at one time."

"Do you think he planned to grow more? That could explain the room he's fitting out with shelving."

"I don't know. And I hate conjecture." Hope righted a chair. "But here's the thing. Until we're in a situation where someone we love is in pain or we're in pain, we have no right to judge."

"I'm not judging. Just surprised, that's all."

Hope tilted her head and stared at Anne.

"Okay, maybe a little." Anne shrugged. "But I don 't mean to judge. Like I said, just surprising."

"I bet if we knew more of the people's lives that they live behind closed doors, we'd really be surprised." Hope laughed.

"Yeah, well, I'd rather not know. Thank you very much." Anne helped Hope right the small tiled table. A piece had broken away and she laid it on a cabinet shelf. "I wonder if Stewart can fix this?"

"Probably. I'll ask him when I go by the Inn today." She found a broom. "Ready?"

Anne took the broom from Hope and started sweeping the flagstone floor while Hope cut back broken limbs and pulled plants that had been uprooted and were a lost cause. They found a few marijuana plants with buds, so Hope took them into the potting area and laid them on the shelf.

They'd been working for a while when they heard voices. Kandi and her brothers had arrived.

Karl carried a basket that probably contained their lunch, while Kevin toted two large jugs of lemonade and tea. Kandi carried a couple of blankets.

"We're here! Ready for a break?"

Anne pulled off her gloves. "Yes. And I'm ready for some of that wonderful lemonade. Greenhouses are nice, but it's a bit like a sauna in there right now."

Karl and Kevin had gone inside to have a look around. They returned as Kandi and Anne were spreading out the blanket on the ground.

"The guy who lives here is seriously hip, man."

Anne glanced over at Hope. They must have found the marijuana plants.

"Actually, his wife is seriously ill, man," Anne replied. "Cancer. Stage Four. Lung."

"Oh, that's lame." Kevin responded.

"I guess that's one way of putting it."

Anne wondered what Kandi had put together for their meal. She pulled out lots of little containers, each with various items such as diced vegetables, seeds, and sliced avocado. A big bowl contained a variety of lettuces and another bowl contained a grain with beans.

"Yum. This is really good. What is it?"

"It's quinoa with pinto beans. I also brought some salsa if you, *like*, want a bit of spice." Kandi handed the container to Anne.

"Keen-wa, huh? Is that with a wa or wah?" Anne took another mouthful.

"It's actually spelled q-u-i-n-o-a, but it's pronounced keen-wa." Kevin added more to his plate.

"You have to love our language. Nothing makes sense." Anne crossed her legs.

"So, how's the work going, and what would you like us to do for you?" Karl laid his plate down on the blanket.

"It's not as bad as I had thought. But there are a few windows that are broken, and another has got a pretty big crack in it that will need to be repaired."

"We can do that. Do you have a tape measure? We can go into town and see if we can find a piece of glass or get it ordered. If it has to be ordered, we can always put a piece of wood there if you want that glass taken down before it falls into the greenhouse and shatters."

"Sounds good. I have to, *like,* get back over to the house and then go by the Inn. A few guests are checking out today, so I want to get those rooms ready for the next guests." Kandi pulled another container from the basket. This one contained all types of fruit.

"Wonderful. Thanks a lot, sweetie. I think that Hope and I can handle it here. We just need to wipe off the doors and other areas that still have the fingerprint dust on it. I might also see if we can get some plants to replace the ones he lost."

Kevin wiped his mouth. "What do you think happened? That he interrupted someone vandalizing his greenhouse?"

"Why do you say——" Of course, if someone had found out that Bill was growing pot, maybe they'd come to grab some. "But who?" Anne spoke more to herself than in answer to Kevin's question.

Kandi flipped her cherry-red hair upside down and piled it on top of her head. Even though Kandi's hair was bright, bottle red, the three siblings all shared the same green eyes, freckled faces and similar shades of red cheeks.

Kandi closed up the basket. "I got a call this morning asking if we had an availability but we're full right now."

"That's a good problem to have." Hope took a sip of her drink and wiped the condensation from her glass.

"Yes. That's true. But I felt, *like*, a bit sorry for her. She said she'd heard how great the Inn was and she wanted to be a bit out from the town."

"Is Sam in town? I know he rents his cabin out when he's away." Hope spoke.

"Oh, that's, *like*, a good idea. I'll give him a call when I get back."

In response to the puzzled looks on the twins' faces, Anne replied, "Sam's an EMT. He's also our deputy coroner."

"He's also got, *like*, the hots for Anne."

"No, he doesn't." Anne grinned and took a sip of lemonade.

"Okay. Whatever." Kandi winked at Anne, who threw a dishtowel back at her.

It was true that Anne and Sam had gone out, but Anne simply wanted to be on her own for a while. It was a nice change to not feel as if she couldn't make it without a man in her life. She'd learned how strong and capable she was, and she didn't want to go back now.

Kevin and Karl stood up at the same time. Karl helped Hope stand while the rest cleaned up their picnic.

A loud male voice interrupted their chatter. "What are you doing here?"

The police officer approached. His hand rested on his gun at his side. "Do you have the right to be here?"

Hope approached him. "Officer, we know Bill and Lori. We came over to clean up the greenhouse before they return."

"Did they give you permission to be here?"

"Well, not exactly. We wanted to do this for them—" Hope continued.

"So, in other words, you're trespassing." He backed up and quickly scanned the group.

Anne stood up. "We're not trespassing. In fact, Sheriff Carson was here earlier, and he's related to them. He allowed us to be here." Okay, a bit of a fib.

"Carson was here?" He glanced toward the greenhouse.

"Yes. He brought Lori's car back for her. It had been in the shop."

"There's been a lot of vandalism in our area recently." He turned to Kandi's brothers. "I don't recall seeing you around here lately."

Karl bristled. "We used to live here. We're Kandi's brothers."

"Do you have identification?"

"Not on us." Kevin moved over next to Karl. "We don't normally carry our passports with us." Under his breath, Anne heard Karl say, "papers please."

She stepped forward before one of the twins did or said something foolish. "Officer," she looked at his badge. "Officer Dale, we didn't want them to have to come back and have to clean up the mess in the greenhouse. Someone attacked Bill as you know. He is still unconscious, and Lori is gravely ill. We're just trying to help them out as good neighbors do." She smiled sweetly and hoped it came across as genuine.

"It doesn't look as if you're helping. It looks like you're enjoying their property without their permission." He nodded at the group. "I think you should leave."

"But—" Anne was losing her patience.

"Certainly, Officer. We'll make sure to get Lori's permission the next time we're here." She put her arm through Anne's. "Come on, Kandi. Boys, can you carry the items?"

They nodded, and the group made their way back to their vehicles.

"The nerve of—" Anne spoke quietly. "He saw us here before. Why is he acting like that now?"

"He's just doing his job. He doesn't know us. I'm sure the police department has a lot on their hands with the increased vandalism, the fires popping up and the school problem."

Anne turned to Hope. "School problem?"

"Spencer stopped by the store today with a few of his friends. I overheard them talking. One of their classmates, a young girl, is in the hospital. It seems she was at a party with a group of friends and they were smoking pot. She'd never tried it before..." Hope shrugged her shoulders and shook her head. "Peer pressure, I guess. Anyway, the joint had been spiked with other drugs. Luckily, the kids realized something was wrong right away and called an ambulance."

"Oh, that's horrible. Growing up, I knew pot was available but it's nothing compared to the drugs kids are exposed to today." She opened the back car door and put in her gloves. "Will she be okay?"

Hope sat down in the passenger seat as Anne slid in behind the wheel. They waved as Kandi and her brothers pulled out. "Yes. They pumped her stomach to be safe and she will have to stay in the hospital for a few days. It will be a hard lesson for her but probably one she won't soon forget."

Anne threw the gear into reverse. She glanced in the rearview camera, where she saw the officer standing by the garage.

He's only doing his job. She had to be thankful for public servants like Officer Dale who made sure all is well. Even if it had meant running them off from a good deed.

Back at the house, Anne kicked off her shoes. She checked on Mouser, who was involved in his daily activity of sleeping on top of the bookcase. Anne headed up the stairs to her bedroom and into the bathroom. In the shower, Anne took her time enjoying the cool spray after being out in the hot sun. She'd just wrapped a towel around herself when she heard her phone trill. It was Kandi.

"Hey, sweetie."

"Hi. Listen, I got back and called Sam. He said Ms. Smith could stay at his place. He's going camping with his scout group this weekend."

"That's good." Anne switched the phone to the other ear.

Anne heard Kandi speak to someone out of earshot. "Sorry. Anyway, here's the thing. He can't show her how to get to his place and he didn't leave a key since he didn't have anyone on the schedule."

"Since when did he start locking his doors?" Anne knew that when she first moved to Carolan Springs, it was rare to find anyone who locked their doors. "And what about Hank?"

"Hank went with him. The boys all love that dog, so they made him an honorary scout member."

Anne could easily visualize the Golden grinning from ear to ear with his vest and badges. "Okay. But that doesn't answer the question about Sam locking his doors."

"He told me that the Bennet's house hadn't been broken into, but the fire marshal said someone went in and started the fire deliberately. With all the fires being set, and his house in such a secluded spot, he decided it would be smart."

"Oh, that's horrible. Do they think either of the Bennetts had anything to do with setting the fire?"

"No. They were visiting family in California, so they've been cleared. But it's scary. I heard through the grapevine that they put the property up for sale—as is. They are leaving for good."

"That's terrible. I hope they don't end up losing money on it, but I would think the land itself is valuable. I guess everyone has to do what they think is best. Knowing someone died in a fire at your house has to be horrible."

"Oh, I bet you haven't seen the paper. Ray Lawrence was killed before the fire was started. He was murdered."

Chapter Nine

Anne returned back to her house and went over to the Brandywine Inn. After checking on the guests, she found Kandi at the desk in the back office.

"When do I need to take this guest over to Sam's?"

"She said she would be coming in tonight, if that would be okay."

Anne nodded. "Yes, I don't have anything else going on, so that works. Did she happen to give you a time?"

Kandi shook her head. "Sorry. She isn't very talkative. Oh wait." She smashed her mouth to the side. "I take it back. She said she'd be here between two thousand and twenty-one hundred. Whatever that means. I guess she means the century." She grinned at Anne.

Anne responded, "It's most likely military time. Two thousand equals eight in the evening and twenty-one hundred is nine o'clock."

Kandi made a face. "What? Then why didn't she just say that?"

"Never mind. It's not something you've heard if you aren't around the military or other services that use it."

"Well, I think it's, *like*, odd. That's all I'm saying about that."

Anne slipped off her shoes and put her feet up under her in the chair. "Did I see your truck leaving earlier?"

"Yes. Kevin asked if he could borrow it, as Autumn is going to go with them to Boulder for some concert or hippie festival or something or other."

Anne wondered if young people today were still considered hippies, once a term from the sixties. Kandi and her brothers certainly looked alike, but other than that, they seemed to be polar opposites.

"I can't believe you let them take your beloved Cherry."

Kandi was extremely proud of the bright red truck that she'd named Cherry.

Kandi grinned. "I told them they could take Cherry as long as they treated her well. It has space for all of them and four wheel drive. Though I doubt they'll need it, unless they head up into the mountains. They are thinking of doing some back country camping if they can find some backpacks and tents to rent."

"I don't know if they'll have much luck with that here in town." Anne rubbed her nose and felt a slight sting. She probably gotten sunburned over at the Connors house. Kandi's face was also slightly pink.

"They're going over to Denver to the REI and also check out the Art Museum while they're in town. They will be back tomorrow to pick up Autumn."

The phone rang. Kandi picked it up, answering in her singsong voice, "Brandywine Inn, how may I help you?"

Anne watched as Kandi's head bounced up and down to whatever the caller was saying. Finally, Kandi responded, "That's, *like*, the best news. See ya."

"What's the best news?" Anne leaned forward in the chair.

"Bill woke up. He's still really groggy, but the doctor says he's going to pull through. Lori's going home and she's doing better—well, as good as, you know."

Anne did know. The prognosis had meant the goal was to make Lori comfortable. The doctor had said she probably only had months. Lori had refused to stay in the hospital for her last days, so in addition to a visiting nurse who came in during the week, Lori was well cared for at home.

"That is good news. We could use some good news with all the bad things happening. I wonder when we can go visit him?"

In answer to Anne's words, Hope answered from the doorway. "I'd say in a day or two. I happened to be there looking in on one of my patients when I saw Lori. She told me about Bill. When I told her about the greenhouse, you should have seen her face. I think she realized we probably would have seen the marijuana plants."

Hope sat down in the adjacent chair. " I explained that we only wanted to help, nothing more. I think she knows that we don't judge her for using it to ease her pain. I told her that Officer Dale had stopped us from finishing and would like to complete the clean-up before Bill returns if that's OK with her. She said it was."

"Great. I can go tomorrow and get some plants to replace the messed-up ones and some flowers for out of the window where Lori sits," Anne responded.

"That sounds nice. I'll go with you." Hope mimicked Anne and also took her shoes off, adjusting her feet across her legs in a yoga pose.

How does she do that? I can barely get one leg on top of the other. Anne tried to put one foot on top of her leg but failed.

Kandi broke the silence. "What about the, you know, the other plants?"

"The other plants?" Anne motioned. Then realization dawned. "Oh, never mind."

She turned to Hope. "Do you know where to get marijuana plants?"

"I'm an herbalist, but I stick to herbs that I'm familiar with and I don't know where to get the actual plants. I bet we could find out from the place that opened up off County Road."

Kandi sat down at the desk and pulled up a web browser. She typed in 'medical marijuana shops Carolan Springs'. "Here it is. Naturaid. Should we give them a call?"

"Yes." Anne replied.

"I'm not going to, *like,* call a pot shop." Kandi held up both hands.

"Oh, geez. Why does the mom have to do everything?" Anne motioned for Kandi to hand her the phone receiver. Once they'd connected, Anne motioned to have the call put on speaker to ask about buying plants. They were disappointed to hear that the organization didn't sell plants.

"OK, well thanks."

The man on the line stopped her. "I think this should be okay since I heard that they will be leaving, but you could check with the Bennetts."

The Bennetts? Anne, Hope and Kandi shared glances with each other.

Anne interjected, "You mean the Bennetts whose house and greenhouse burned down?"

"Yep. Sad. But I think that they have a small grow-room away from it that could still have some plants."

The man said something to another person. "I've got to go. Come in if you have more questions."

Anne, Hope and Kandi sat in silence. Ray Lawrence have been selling drugs to teens. The Bennetts had been growing marijuana. The Connors had some plants in the greenhouse.

They all had a connection to drugs. Was there a dangerous vigilante on the loose?

Chapter Ten

Kandi broke the spell that had come over all of them. "What should we, *like*, do?"

"Do about what?" Hope stretched her arms over her head. "We don't really have anything other than the facts that these things occurred. But there may be no connection between them at all."

"True. But we all agree that it seems like too much of a coincidence, doesn't it?" Anne grimaced at Hope's flexibility. Just looking at her made Anne's arms hurt.

Hope uncrossed her legs. "I can't see taking this to the police. What could they do with it?"

Anne looked over to see Kandi raise her cellphone to her ear. "Can I speak with Sheriff Carson?"

Anne held her hands up with a "what are you doing?" look.

Kandi stuck up her hand in a stop motion. "Yes, okay. Well, would you tell him to call me or he can stop by the Brandywine Inn if he's on this side of town?" She listened. "Okay, thanks. Bye, Ms. Thelma."

Anne remembered the no-nonsense woman from the time she'd spend at the police station. She wouldn't want to be on that woman's bad side.

It was only a short time later that they heard a vehicle pull up and looked out to see the sheriff's car. He pulled in on Anne's driveway instead of the adjoining gravel drive used by the Inn's guests.

Anne met the sheriff once he'd arrived at the door. "Ms. Freemont."

"Sheriff."

When she turned back, she saw Kandi roll her eyes at Hope. They could make fun all they liked. From now on, they were only the local sheriff and the local innkeeper. An image of her pressing her lips to his popped quickly to mind. Nope, that had been a spur-of-the-moment thing to avoid a disaster. It was a mistake. That's it.

Hope rose from her chair. "Sheriff." She shook his hand. "Here, please. Take my seat."

She pulled up a stool from the corner and sat down.

After they had shared their suspicions, he leaned back and shut his notebook. "This is what you called me over here for?"

"There's, *like*, a lot of things that are, *like*, too coincidental. All the fires, and Spencer said Ray was *like* selling to the fosters, and, *like*…"

Carson held up his hand. "Thanks. But what do you think I should do with this information? While the issue over at the Bennetts is under the sheriff's purview, the attack on Bill is under the police department."

Anne spoke up. "We figured if we told you, then you could go to Chief Everett with it."

"So, I should go to Police Chief Everett with 'it'?"

"Yes," Anne and Kandi chimed.

Anne looked at Hope, who remained silent. Why wasn't she chiming in?

"And when I go to the chief I will say, 'Hey, I think there's a bad guy out there doing bad things.'"

Anne and Kandi's faces fell.

"Well, of course not." Anne crossed her arms defiantly. "But couldn't you share that there could be some DNA evidence or other things that could tie all the crimes together?"

"Okay. And …?"

Anne bristled. "Look, we're just trying to help here. You could be a little bit more thankful we're helping make your job easier."

"You're making my job easier?"

"Argh. Stop answering my statements with questions," Anne huffed.

Hope rose from the stool. "Sheriff, we do know what it sounds like. But we didn't know if there were anything that might be of some importance that could add to the investigation."

"You're right, Hope," he replied.

Why does he call her Hope? Anne sighed loudly. Hope and Sheriff Carson turned toward her.

"Something you'd like to add, Ms. Freemont?" He cocked his head toward her.

"No. We've said what we need to say."

"Okay, well thank you for the information." He stood and readjusted his gear belt.

"Let me see you out, Sheriff." Anne stressed the last word.

They opened the office door and a tall, slim woman with her hair pulled tightly back against her head stood in the hall. She wore black from head to toe and no makeup.

"I'm Mary Smith. I came to get directions to—" She pulled a piece of paper from her pocket. "Sam's house."

Anne shook her hand. "I'll be the one taking you out there."

"Ms. Smith." Carson tipped his Stetson.

"Did I interrupt something? Nothing bad has happened, I hope?"

"No. All's well." He turned back to Kandi and Hope. "I'll be leaving now. Call me if you have any more …facts … in the case."

"A case? That sounds a bit scary," the woman replied with a questioning face.

"Not to worry. It's all under control." He tipped his hat at Anne and left.

"If you would like something to drink, I'll just be a few minutes and we can go," Anne said to the woman. Anne glanced at the clock. It was earlier than the woman said she'd arrive.

"That sounds nice. It was a bit of a drive here. But I got here a bit sooner than I anticipated."

Kandi hopped over and said, "I'll take you into the dining room. We have drinks and snacks in there."

As they walked away, Anne wondered why the woman hadn't knocked and how much of their conversation she'd heard. Her words and her demeanor didn't seem to match. Maybe it was because of being in the military. But something nagged at Anne's mind. Why had Carson said it was all under control when it clearly wasn't?

Chapter Eleven

Anne had driven the woman out to Sam's place. Without Hank bounding out to greet her with his huge doggy grin, the cabin seemed lonely. She found the key where Sam had instructed and let Mary inside. She showed her to the guest room, which faced the lake.

"It's beautiful here." Mary set her bag down on the bed.

"Yes, Sam has a great place here." Anne joined the woman over by the large picture windows.

Anne showed her the trailhead where she could walk or run and pointed in the direction of their houses. "If you'd like to come up for breakfast, you're more than welcome. It's a nice walk, about four miles, with no real elevation gain."

"I may take you up on that. What time do you serve breakfast?"

"Continental starts at seven and full breakfast at eight."

Anne said goodnight and headed home. As she reached her drive, she spied Kandi waving at her from the porch of the Inn. Anne exited the vehicle as Kandi joined her. Anne could tell by Kandi's expression that something was wrong.

"What's the matter, sweetie? Is everything okay?" She took hold of Kandi's arms and could feel the shaking.

"I can't believe it. I mean, *like,* I can believe it. But seriously, *like*, what… I can't believe it!"

"You want to come inside and tell me what this is all about?"

Kandi nodded, and Anne could see tears in the young woman's eyes. Something had clearly upset her.

Anne unlocked the door to the kitchen and was greeted by Mouser giving her a big meow. "Hello, you. I've missed you too." Anne scratched behind his ear the way he liked it and the purring commenced. "Grab a seat, Kandi."

Kandi plopped down on a chair as Anne set Mouser down on the floor. He wound around her legs a few times, hopped up on a nearby ledge, and began grooming himself.

Anne waited, her hands folded in front of her on the table.

Kandi composed herself. "My brothers. They almost got arrested today! They think that since they're in Colorado, they can have as much pot as they want." She stiffened. "And in my truck. How could they do that?"

"What happened?" Anne got up from her chair and set about making a chamomile tea for them.

"They'd come back from Denver and they'd picked up some pot. Then they smoked some, I guess." She looked up at Anne. "I don't get the attraction. I've never liked any kind of smoking."

"Well, it is a bit different, and who am I to judge when I enjoy a glass of wine now and again." Anne poured water into the teakettle.

"I guess. It's just never held any appeal for me."

"I hear you. It's never appealed to me either, but I'm not sure I wouldn't try it if I found out I was deathly ill and dealing with pain constantly like Lori."

"True. I suppose you don't know, do you?" She straightened up. "But they're doing it to, *like*, get high. And then driving MY truck. I'm so mad I could, *like*, spit."

"I think you just did." Anne pretended to wipe her face.

Kandi grinned. "Okay, I'll settle down." She leaned back in the chair. "But don't you think I have a right to be upset?"

"Definitely. Driving under the influence of anything is irresponsible."

"They swore they had done it long before they got behind the wheel but I'm still angry. Plus, now Officer Dale is going to think I'm a pothead." She clenched her teeth.

"Why would he think that?" Anne poured the hot water over the herbs.

"Well, he stopped them for speeding and then he had to know it was my truck."

"What happened exactly?"

"I guess he smelled it—"

"Yes, it's a pretty distinctive smell." Anne set a cup in front of Kandi.

"That gave him cause or something to search the truck. He made them stand back by his cruiser and he went through all their stuff."

"He found some then?"

"Yes, I think over thirty grams, which is over the limit, but he gave them a warning as they said it was for both of them."

"Well, I'm sure they learned their lesson." Anne strained the tea and poured some into each of their cups.

"The weird thing is they looked really upset when they told me. I mean more than just getting caught. I don't know why but when I asked them, they said to stay out of it for my own good. What do you think they meant by that?"

"They're probably embarrassed that they got you involved in the situation," Anne added a teaspoon of honey to her cup. Then she took some and popped the spoon in her mouth. "Oh man, I love Bill's honey. It is so good."

Kandi nodded her head. "It sure is. He wins the top prize almost every year."

"Are your brothers still going to Boulder then?"

"If they are, they're not taking my truck to do it."

A knock at the door startled the pair. Anne stood up and saw Stewart waving at them. Anne opened the door and Stewart came in.

"Tea?" Anne asked.

"No, thanks." He turned to Kandi. "Are you still going to be able to go with me to Ray's funeral tomorrow?"

"Yes. Oh, I just remembered." She turned to Anne. "Lori would like us to stop by tomorrow. I'm trying to figure out how to do that and make it to the funeral on time."

Stewart spoke, "Anne, why don't you come with us? I can drive you out to Bill and Lori's and then we can all leave from there. Bill had asked me to look into putting some more electricity in his greenhouse, so I can look at that while you all are visiting."

"That works for me." Anne yawned loudly. "I better get to bed. You know us old-fogies have to get our sleep."

Kandi came over and gave Anne a peck on the cheek. "Night, Mom."

"Stewart, I know you'll walk my girl home safely, right?"

"Yes." He nodded.

Kandi rolled her eyes at Anne. It was evident that Anne's ploy to get her and Stewart together was no longer a secret. Yet, she crooked her arm in his and smiled up sweetly at him. "Okay, lead on, valiant knight."

Anne waved them good night from her porch and then stepped back into her kitchen. She locked the door. Would it be nice to have her very own valiant knight?

Mouser meowed.

"Yes, yes, I have you." She picked him up and headed up to bed.

Chapter Twelve

Anne knew the service would be casual, so she had put on a flowery dress with white-heeled sandals. She'd recently had her auburn hair cut into a layered style, so she left it flowing freely over her shoulders. The sunburn on her face had faded, and she rubbed coconut oil into it, giving her a healthy glow. She slathered on a pinky-peach lipstick and took a glance in the mirror. She blew an air kiss at her reflection.

It was funny that she had become so much happier with the way she looked now. Years ago, when she'd been married to Duke, she was model-thin, had hair extensions and wore dresses that cost more than many of the Carolan Springs residents' yearly salary. Now she was heavier but healthier, and her natural beauty shone out. She'd had money, prestige, all the things that people think they want, and she had been miserable. Now she had a daughter, friends who loved her and that weren't like those who talked about her the minute her back had been turned. She could spend as much time as she wanted out with her hands in the dirt and spend the evenings, not at a fancy-dress party, but sitting on the porch swinging and doing absolutely nothing.

Life was simpler. For that, Anne was grateful. Well, it would be if these bad things would quit happening. First, finding her neighbor dead and then a murder the weekend they opened the Brandywine Inn. Now all the fires and an influx of drugs into the community. She frowned, wondering what could be done about it.

Anne had made it downstairs when her front doorbell rang. Who could that be? Most people she knew used the back door. She looked through the peephole. Sheriff Carson.

Anne opened the door. "Sheriff Carson. To what do I owe the pleasure?"

He stared at her for a moment. "Do you time to speak to me? I have some questions about the information you all shared with me the other day."

"Sorry, no. I'm going out to see the Connors, and then we're going to Ray's funeral."

He pulled his hat off and held it in his hands. Anne noticed one piece of hair sticking up on his head and forced herself not to reach up and push it back into place.

"Yes, Spencer told me that was today. Are you going by yourself?"

"No. I'm going with Kandi and Stewart."

"Okay. Listen…"

"Yes?"

"I heard about Kandi's brothers."

"Well, they're young. I'm sure you did things you didn't think through when you were their age."

He said nothing.

"Or maybe you didn't." Anne crossed her arms in front of her chest. "We can wait out here if you want." She joined him on the front porch. He leaned against the porch beam.

"I know you're going to the Connors and now to Ray's funeral. You're like someone with a bee in her bonnet. You don't let things go. Let this go. You could get hurt."

"I don't know what you're talking about."

"I think you do. Stay out of it. If not for your sake, then for Kandi's."

"That almost sounds like a threat." She gripped the sides of her arms as a shiver coursed through her. Was it from the shade of the porch or from what he'd said?

"You're not invincible. You're not a professional. Your snooping will cause someone to get hurt. Or worse, killed."

His tone and words shocked her. "It must be awfully lonely on that high moral ground you stand on." Yikes, what had caused her to say that?

"Don't forget that I tried to warn you." He hit his hat against his knee.

Warn me? A real shiver ran down Anne's spine.

She watched as he put his hat back on his head and descended the steps. As she moved to close the door, he turned around. "You look very nice today, Anne." He tipped his head and left.

Anne shut the door, more conflicted than ever.

Sitting in Bill and Lori's living room, Anne asked Lori how she was doing.

"I'm holding up." She pulled the coverlet on her legs into her hand, her grip belying her statement.

"Ms. Conner, I hope you don't mind me being, *like*, rude, but it sure doesn't seem that way to me."

Kandi's words must have hit home as Lori broke down sobbing uncontrollably.

"Please." Anne reached over and knelt in front of the crying woman. "We're here to help. That's all."

Anne consoled Lori as Kandi sprinted back into the room and handed over a wad of toilet paper.

Lori looked up and accepted it, her hand bearing the bruises of the pinpricks from her hospital IV. "I just don't know." She shook her head. "But I have to talk to someone. It might as well be you." She sucked in a deep breath and composed herself.

"How about a cup of coffee or tea? I'd be happy to make some." Anne offered.

"I'll do it!" Kandi hopped up from her spot.

"You're so sweet, Kandi. Thank you." Lori wiped her nose with the tissues. "I think I'd like some Darjeeling."

"Me too," Anne responded. "She is a sweetie. Thanks, Kandi."

Kandi beamed at the praise.

They were sitting in the same sunroom where Anne had seen Lori the day of the beehive tour. "I think that fella has a crush on that girl."

Anne watched as Stewart pulled a piece of broken glass from the greenhouse and put it into a garbage bin. "Yes, I agree. I don't want to push Kandi, but I think they'd make a good match."

"People are often blind when it comes to who's the right person for them. They look for something else when the very thing they need is often right in front of them."

Anne nodded. "Any relationship is not one to be rushed, I guess."

"Yes, but if I'd have known this stupid cancer would come into our lives, I would have married Bill much sooner."

"I'm sorry. That had to be a shock." Anne stood as Kandi came in bearing a tray with cups, cream, and sugar. After everyone had doctored their tea, Lori took a tentative sip.

"After my diagnosis, we didn't know what to do. So many options, treatments—each sounding worse than the others. I didn't want to live my last days stuck hooked up to machines and visiting doctors every week. If I was going to die, I wanted to do it in my own way."

She took another sip of the tea.

"Bill knew when I made up my mind, I wouldn't change it. But he wouldn't give up. He read up on alternative therapies." She stopped and glanced over to Anne.

Anne patted Lori's hand. "Look, we know what you had in the greenhouse. It's not our place, nor would we judge anyone."

Lori smiled at Anne. Then she laughed. It stopped when a fit of coughing took over. Anne took Lori's cup and set it on the table next to her.

The woman winced as she held a hand over her chest. "I'm okay. It's not a fun disease. At first, I could handle the pain with pills or patches, but it got worse. A lot worse. At that point, I told Bill I'd try anything. He heard about people helping the pain through marijuana, so I said I'd try it. It helped, but I needed more than what I could buy as we'd started juicing it into smoothies. Then Bill decided that he'd grow some in the greenhouse."

Anne nodded and sipped her tea. She listened as Lori continued.

"I actually began feeling better and I could get out of bed. It's so much nicer in here, where I can look outside, so Bill wanted to convert one of the potting shed areas at the back of the greenhouse to grow more plants."

Lori shivered, and Kandi pulled a shawl from the back of her chair and wrapped it around the thin woman's frame. "I don't know if that's when things started getting…" She became lost in thought.

"Started getting what?" Anne urged.

The woman looked up. "Bill had to see about more plants. He talked to … um, Ben, or—"

"Bennett?"

"Yes, that's it. Do you know him?" Lori asked Anne.

"No." Anne shot Kandi a look to not say anything about the burning down of the Bennett homestead or about Ray being found dead in the greenhouse.

"It was like something had changed. Bill's demeanor." She shook her head and pulled the shawl tighter.

"Do you mean from doing marijuana?"

"Oh, no. Bill would never use recreationally. It's just not his thing. But as he saw me feeling better, he said we should try cannabinoid oil. It's more potent and some people have reacted well to it."

"That sounds like something a husband would want for his wife," Anne replied.

Lori nodded. "Yes, but it's not cheap. It's pretty expensive to purchase and with Bill cutting back on his job to care for me, money's been tight. I had to quit my job, and the only reason he keeps his is to ensure we have medical insurance."

Anne wondered how the pair were making ends meet when Lori interrupted her thoughts.

"This," Lori waved her hands around, indicating the room. "It's how we're surviving. We took out an equity loan. I didn't want to do it, but Bill said not to worry, that he'd found a way to generate a good income and we could pay off the loan soon."

"Did he say what it was?" Anne replied.

"No. He said I had enough on my shoulders. That I only needed to worry about getting well." She looked at her now empty cup.

Kandi popped up from her seat. "Let me put more water on to heat."

Lori leaned forward in her chair. "I'm worried, Anne. Something's going on and this attack on Bill proves it. No way it was simple vandalism. Someone meant to hurt Bill. I don't know why. But it has me scared now too."

"Now too?"

"Bill came home not too long ago, and I'd never seen him look the way he did. He was angry but also afraid. It's something I've never seen in all the years we've been married."

Kandi had returned, and they refilled cups with the warming tea. She plopped down in her chair and then waved. Stewart stood outside and motioned to his watch. He'd said he'd give them a twenty-minute warning before they needed to leave.

"How is Bill doing?" Anne sipped the delicious tea.

"He's doing better. The doctor has said he's out of the woods and should be able to come home in the next few days. But that's why I'm worried."

"Why?" Anne motioned for Kandi to clear up the dishes.

"Because he told me the first thing he wanted to do when he got out was to go buy a gun."

Chapter Thirteen

The crowd was small as they gathered around the gravesite. Mrs. Lawrence wept silently into her handkerchief as a group of foster teens stood sullenly behind her. Anne caught Spencer's eye and he nodded acknowledgment.

Anne surveyed the rest of the group. Mainly people from the town she didn't know. Strangely, the Bennetts weren't attending, even though Ray's body had been found in their greenhouse. They had to have known him.

She also noticed Officer Dale standing apart from the crowd, leaning against his police cruiser.

What was that old saying about the killer coming back to the scene of the crime? This certainly wasn't the scene of the crime, but maybe Officer Dale was seeing who showed up at Ray's funeral.

Was the killer here?

Her gaze moved across the group. She didn't know many of the people, so there was no way to know who might have wished harm to Ray Lawrence.

She looked up to see that Police Chief Everett had joined Officer Dale. The pair stood as sentinels next to their vehicles. Why had they come? It was a small town, but it seemed strange to see the pair. Anne turned as she heard a sob being stifled. It was the Bennetts. When had they arrived?

"Ashes to ashes," the pastor intoned.

A cry escaped Mrs. Bennett's lips. Anne watched as the pair turned and quickly strode away from the scene. If Ray had been killed, had the Bennetts been the intended victims? If so, why? Anne turned back to see that Everett had left and only Officer Dale remained.

The service broke up and Anne made her way over to the policeman while Kandi and Stewart stayed behind, waiting to pay their respects.

"Hello, Officer Dale."

He bent his head down to look at her. "Yes?"

"I'm Anne Fremont."

He didn't respond.

"I know that you're working the vandalism case over at the Connors. I'm just wondering if that case and Ray's death aren't connected."

He stiffened. "What do you mean?"

"Well, we tried to talk to Sheriff Carson—"

"You've spoken to Sheriff Carson about this?"

"Well, we—"

"Who's we?"

Something niggled at the back of her mind, but Anne ignored it. "Hope and Kandi."

"Go on." He pushed his sunglasses back up his nose.

"Well, he said that we had no proof—"

"Proof of what?"

"Of the cases being related."

"I think that it would be best if you came into the police station and we can take down your statement."

"Do you think I did the right thing by coming to you?"

"Oh yes, you did the right thing."

Anne turned as she heard Kandi call out her name. "Coming!"

Officer Dale got in his car and drove off. As he did, Anne looked up, and to her surprise, found the guest that was staying at Sam's place watching the scene. Anne walked over to the woman. Had she also been standing there during the funeral?

"Hello," Anne called out to the woman.

The woman approached. She was wearing blue jeans and a tank top, but it was covered by a chambray shirt, the sleeves rolled up to the elbow. Her hair was in its same tightly pulled-back bun. "Hello."

"I have to say, we have lots of interesting places to see in town, but I probably wouldn't consider the cemetery one of them."

"It's a hobby of mine. I go to cemeteries to see the older headstones. Usually, they're eighteen hundred but trying to find earlier ones." She nodded toward the freshly dug grave. "Is that the funeral for the man found in the burned-out greenhouse?"

Anne started. "Yes. How did you know about that?"

"I read it in the paper. It was at Sam's place." She pushed imaginary hairs off her face and in that moment, Anne caught a glimpse of a concealed weapon.

Who was this woman? Why was she here at the cemetery? Why was she carrying a gun?

Certainly, lots of people were concealed carriers but not usually when it was someone visiting from out of state.

"I need to get back to the others. They're waiting on me and I'm riding with them."

"You know I found some old clippings. Something about you helping solve a case or something?"

Anne laughed but it came out flat. "Oh, our silly town newspaper has nothing else to write about, so they try to sensationalize the little they have to work with. I really better be off. Good seeing you."

She made to walk away when the woman grabbed her arm. Startled, Anne turned back to face the woman.

"Be safe. You don't want to get involved in things you don't understand." The woman dropped Anne's arm and strode away.

What in the—? Anne rubbed the place where the woman had tightly gripped her arm. Then she walked quickly to join Kandi and Stewart.

Chapter Fourteen

"What do you mean she had, *like,* a gun?" Kandi's voice rose as they made their way indoors.

Hope interjected, "She threatened you? What exactly did she say?"

"I'm telling you. She was standing over by a tree, so I thought I'd say hi. She raised her arm and her shirt came open and that's when I saw the gun. Then she told me to be safe and not get involved. Involved in what?"

"I don't know, but something strange is going on." Hope raised up her fingers. "One, the fires. Lots of little ones being set around town. Why and who's behind it? Two. The big fire out at the Bennetts. Is that the same arsonist or someone else? What was Ray doing at the Bennetts and why did someone kill him? Are the killer and the arsonist the same person?"

Anne interjected, "Or did they think it was one of the Bennetts? I heard at the funeral that only his wife had planned to go out of town, and he joined her at the last minute."

"They're moving," Kandi spoke up.

"What do you mean?" Hope turned to Kandi.

"They, *like*, told their neighbor they'd sold the property 'as-is' and were leaving."

Normally, Anne would have asked how Kandi knew that, but in this town, nothing stayed secret for long.

"Okay, back to our list." Hope held up her hand. "Recap—the woman at Sam's with a gun, telling you to stay out of something. Next, Ray Lawrence killed. The Bennett's place burned down. Why? To cover the murder? Three, someone attacks Bill, and his greenhouse wrecked."

Kandi tucked a lock of hair behind her ear. "We need to, *like,* talk to Sheriff Carson."

Anne shook her head. "Nope. He said we don't have any facts or proof. I've already talked with Officer Dale and he said I should come into the station and talk with them. He's taking this far more seriously than Carson is doing. Plus, Carson told me to stay out of it."

"I don't know. There are just too many variables."

"Too many what?" Kandi turned on the light, dispelling the gloom from the room.

"Basically, we have lots of questions and no answers." Anne sighed. "I guess this is one time we can't figure out what's going on."

"You think, ND?"

Anne started. Sheriff Carson stood in the doorway. How long had he been standing there? Long enough for him to hear her talk about him? She felt the hot flush of embarrassment creep into her face.

He held up his hand. "For your information, I do take this seriously. In fact, I take this very seriously. More so than you know. But I also know how you three are. So far things have turned out okay, but that's not always going to be the case. You need to know when to back off your meddling."

"Meddling?" Anne hopped up and stood toe to toe with Carson. "Meddling! I'm so tired of you constantly demeaning me."

"I'm not demeaning you. I know that you're a smart, capable woman."

Anne's anger fizzled, and she backed up.

He held up his hand. "However, I also know I don't want to see you…" He gave a quick nod to Hope and Kandi. "Or them, get hurt. Know your limits. You need to step away from this."

Hope spoke, "Sheriff. There's definitely something going on that we're missing. And what you're saying is good advice." She spoke to Carson, but she gazed over at Anne. "We're not invincible as much as we all think we are."

"Fine. Even you're not on my side anymore," Anne huffed.

"It has nothing to do with sides. I know we have to be realistic here. Sometimes we don't know what we don't know."

Anne retorted, "Okay, fine. But will you at least hear us out? Officer Dale is interested in what I have to say."

"Officer Dale, huh?" Carson turned back to Anne. "What did he say?"

"That I should come into the police station and tell them everything I thought."

"Like?" he countered.

"Like Ray dealing drugs and then he's killed, and Bill hit on the head and the Bennetts leaving and the woman carrying a gun—"

"Whoa. What?"

Kandi joined in. "Anne says the woman staying at Sam's had a gun at the cemetery at Ray's funeral."

Carson turned back to Anne. "What woman? She had a gun? She was at Ray's funeral?"

"See. That's what I mean. I know things."

The phone rang, interrupting the debate between Carson and Anne.

Hope picked it up, listened and screamed out, "Oh, no!"

"What is it?"

"Someone set my shop on fire!"

Chapter Fifteen

"I'll drive. Come on." Anne grabbed her keys as Hope rushed past her out the back door. Kandi starting crying, and Carson said he'd help her home.

Anne pushed past the speed limit to get to town while Hope was on the phone trying to get through to Autumn. "Autumn, this is Hope, please pick up. Call me!" Her voice grew more frantic.

"Is your mom at home alone?"

"Yes. I told Autumn that I wouldn't be long, and as long as Mom is in front of her favorite show, she doesn't move until it's finished." She buried her head in her hands. "Oh, Mom. Mom. I'll never forgive myself…"

They arrived to see a firetruck outside of the store. The window in the front was completely gone, but no fire seemed to be coming out of the window—only thick, black smoke.

From around the back, Anne watched as a frail older woman emerged.

"Mama!" Hope cried out, running over and embracing the woman.

"It's okay, baby. Don't cry." She patted Hope's head.

An EMT came over and began checking Faith. "Ma'am, are you okay? Are you hurt anywhere?"

"Hurt? Why would I be hurt?"

"Because of the fire. Did you get burned?"

"Fire? Where's a fire?" She glanced toward the front and saw the black smoke. "Is there a fire? I hope no one is in the fire."

Hope stole a look at Anne. Her mother's dementia had taken hold. Had Faith accidentally started the fire?

A firefighter came over as the EMT led Faith to the waiting ambulance. "Ma'am, is this your store?" he spoke to Hope.

She nodded. "Yes."

"I think we caught it before it could get too bad. You've lost anything that was close to the window, but it could have been a lot worse. Thankfully someone called it in."

"They saw it on fire?" Anne wrapped her arm around Hope.

"At first, they thought it was a trick of the light, so they didn't do anything. But then they thought they'd drive back by it. That's when they noticed that the door in the alley for the store entrance had been broken. They called in the police, as they thought it might be a burglary."

"What started it?" Hope fought back tears.

"Looks to be some type of incendiary device."

"What!" Hope and Anne exclaimed in unison.

"Yes, but I have to wait for the fire marshal to give a ruling on it. But it wasn't an accident." He walked back to his crew as they began the process of putting all their gear away.

"Who would want to do such a thing? Why? Why? My mother could have been killed." Hope broke down, weeping silently.

As Anne comforted her friend, the words haunted her: "I don't want you to get hurt, or Hope or Kandi, or someone get killed." Did Carson know anything about this?

A hand landed on her shoulder and Anne jumped. It was Spencer. "What's going on?"

"Hope had a fire in her store. It doesn't look to be too bad, but it's still upsetting."

"For sure. Did they catch, you know, who did it?"

"No. We just got here, and they'll only be starting the investigation—wait, what do you mean 'who did it'? How do you know it wasn't an accident?"

"I overheard some kids talking at Ms. Lawrence's the night after the funeral. One said they were going to make some quick money and score some weed by doing an easy job."

"I don't see how this relates to the fire in Hope's shop."

"He went on to say that all he had to do was break into a shop and leave a package. It had to be during a certain time at night."

"You mean tonight?"

Spencer nodded his head. "Yes."

Anne took hold of Spencer's arm. "We've got to find this kid. He knows who set him up to do it. You need to tell the police."

Spencer shook his head. "I don't think so. I don't want to end up, you know, six-feet-under like Ray."

"Why would you say that?"

Spencer's agitation grew. "You wouldn't believe me if I told you."

"Look, we've got to find this kid right away and we have to know what he said. This is serious. Hope's mom could have been killed."

"You're not going to like it. I don't know. I—" Spencer moaned.

Hope grabbed Spencer. "Spit it out. What did he say?"

Spencer jerked back at Hope's force. "He said it was the sheriff. The sheriff paid him."

Anne clutched at her throat. She felt sick to her stomach. No. It couldn't' be. He wouldn't go that far to make a point. Before she knew what was happening, gentle arms were lowering her to a seated position on the side of the curb. The tears fell with a low keening that turned to sobbing. Not caring what anyone thought, Anne felt as if her heart had been shattered into a million pieces. It couldn't be true. It couldn't. Not after she 'd opened her heart up again. She rocked back and forth.

After the emotions had run their course, a hand came into view. It held a package of tissues. She looked up to see Police Chief Everett standing over her. "May I?"

She nodded yes. Anne opened the package and wiped her eyes and nose. She felt drained and cold.

"I... sorry, I don't know what came over me."

"A lot of people can have emotional experiences when something tragic happens." He bent down on one knee. "Are you up for answering some questions?"

"Yes. But I don't know how I can help. I got here at the same time as Hope." Anne realized that, in her emotional outburst, she'd lost sight of Hope and Spencer. "Where's..."

"Ms. Boswell is with her mother. They're being checked over by the med techs."

Anne hugged her knees. "I'll tell you what I can."

"Great." He pulled out a long notebook similar to the one Carson used.

Anne fought back a new surge of tears. She bit her lip.

"Can you tell me where you were when the fire started?" He hit the plunger on the pen, readying himself to write.

"We…"

"We?" He interrupted.

"Me, Kandi and Hope were over at the Inn. We were talking about…"

"So just you three?"

"Yes. Um, no. Carson, I mean, Sheriff Carson came in."

"What time was that? Do you remember?"

"No."

"Had you called him to the Inn?"

"No."

"He just showed up without you calling him?"

"Yes."

She watched as he made notes. Why had Carson come there? To warn them off again?

"Then Ms. Boswell received a call about her shop?"

"Yes."

"Who called her?"

"I don't know."

"It's okay. I know this is difficult. Just take your time." His voice was soothing, and Anne relaxed.

"Hope got the call and then we rushed over here."

"Great." He nodded while writing. "You got here and what happened next?"

"The fire was out, but smoke was still coming out of the building. Hope was worried about her mom, who lives with her."

"Go on." He laid his hand next to the notepad.

"Then someone found Faith."

"Did you talk to anyone else?"

She turned to him. "Only to Spencer."

"Spencer?"

"Yes. He came to see what was happening."

"That name sounds familiar. That isn't Spencer Andrews?"

"Yes. Do you know him?"

"I'm often stopping over to see about the foster kids at the Lawrence's. She does a great job for those kids in our town."

"Yes."

"Did Spencer say anything to you?" He held his pen poised.

"Say anything? Like what?" Alarms were ringing in Anne's head as she remembered Carson's words: you don't want anyone to get hurt. Hope's shop had been vandalized and her mother could have been killed. She wasn't going to put Spencer in any cross-hairs.

"He wanted to make sure we were okay. That's all."

"Okay, good." He pulled out his card and handed it to her. If you think of anything else, you let me know." He got up from his position and headed toward the ambulance where Hope stood outside, and Faith sat on a stretcher. Spencer was nowhere to be seen.

She heard Faith's voice, "It was that young man. He helped me out of the house and took me away for a walk. He brought me ice cream. I like ice cream."

"Did this nice young man tell you his name, ma'am?" Police Chief Everett inquired.

"Yes, he had a strange name." Faith's head bobbed up and down.

"Do you remember what it was?" He spoke soft and soothing tones like how he'd spoken to Anne.

"It was the funniest thing. Sheriff. He said his name was Sheriff." She laughed.

Chapter Sixteen

Anne fought sleep that night. She finally fell asleep only to have crazy dreams involving fires, and pot, and black cancer that grew and grew with no way to stop its advance. She cried out and fought, flames starting on every side, running, running…

A soft paw tapped her nose. Another touch. She tried not to open her eyes, to see how long Mouser would keep at it. But even through her squint, he saw she was awake. "Meow."

"Feed me. Feed me. You're like that scary shop of horrors plant. It's all about you, isn't it?" Mouser looked at her and meowed again as if to say, "Yes, so?"

Anne reached up and patted his head as she heard a ping sound. Ahhh, the treat tray had opened. Mouser jumped off the bed and headed to the bathroom where Anne kept another tray, in case she forgot to fill the one up downstairs before going to bed. "I see how you are. You only love me when it's convenient."

Anne turned over and pulled the covers up to her neck. She closed her eyes, willing herself to keep any thoughts at bay. Maybe she could go back to sleep. But the events of last night kept flooding back. After they'd cleared Faith and Hope, Kandi had offered to let them stay at her house. Her grandfather's room had been on the first floor when it was his house and Kandi had kept it as a guest room. It would be easier on Faith than having to climb stairs at the Inn or at Anne's.

Anne flipped over and stared at the ceiling. Her goal in moving to Carolan Springs had been to enjoy the simple life, but it had been anything but since she'd arrived. She kept running the events on replay in her mind. Over and over. Something was trying to get her attention and she just couldn't grab it.

She yelled out to the ether, "What is it?"

Whatever the elusive thing was, it wasn't wanting to make its presence known. Frustrated at not being able to go back to sleep or to put two thoughts together that made any sense, Anne flung the covers back and sat on the edge of the bed. She looked at the clock.

That can't be right.

She picked it up and looked closer. Ten. She couldn't remember the last time she'd slept that late.

She set the clock back down and shoved her feet into slippers. Pulling on a soft fuzzy robe, she headed downstairs to make some coffee.

She'd just taken her first sip of coffee when she heard her phone ringing. It was Kandi.

"Hullo?" She took another swig of coffee.

"Where have you been?" Kandi's voice was frantic. "I've been calling and calling. Why didn't you answer your phone?"

"Sorry. I left it downstairs and I slept in. What's the matter, honey? Did I forget something I needed to do at the Inn?"

"No. No. It's nothing like that. You need to get over here."

"Why?"

"They've arrested Sheriff Carson."

The cup fell from Anne's hand and smashed on the floor. As she looked down, coffee pooled at her feet. She gripped the sink.

She heard Kandi's voice as if through a fog, "Mom! Anne. Mom, are you okay?"

"I'm fine." She canceled the call.

She began laughing hysterically. "I'm fine," she said aloud. "Isn't that what every woman says when they're not fine?" The tears came again. She didn't know why she was crying. Maybe her hormones were acting up again. Maybe she was tired. Or maybe... no, she wouldn't consider that.

She bent down and began picking up the broken pieces.

~

Over at Kandi's, Anne found Hope, Faith, and Stewart sitting around the kitchen table. Cups were in front of them and a good portion of a coffeecake was missing.

Kandi ran over and hugged Anne. "Are you okay?"

"Yes. I just slept in." Anne returned the hug.

She walked over to Hope and gave her a hug too. "How are you doing? Were you able to get any sleep last night?"

"Yes. I took a stress aid tincture and it helped me."

"I think I should get some of that." Anne poured herself a cup of coffee, then joined the group at the table.

Stewart rose from his chair. "I best be going. I'm going out to the Connors to install the new glass and then going over to check out the new event center going up at the Bennett's old place.

"What?"

"That's what I thought. Fast, right? They've already got trucks out bulldozing the remains of the greenhouse and they were able to save quite a bit of the house. They're going to make it into an event ranch. A big barn is going up and they're going to have places for RVs and campsites, so they're putting in a ton of amperage for all the power they'll need. Then the Bennett's old house will be joined by a couple of other houses for overnight guests and entertainers."

"That's a huge plan. I'm surprised that got put through with permits and stuff." Hope set her cup down.

"Really? I think all you need is some money and things get passed pretty easy." Stewart huffed.

Hope sighed. "Corruption can be found anywhere, I guess."

Stewart rose to leave. "Later." He smiled at Kandi, who returned his smile.

"Want an omelet? It's almost, *like*, time for lunch anyway. We could do brunch."

Anne sat down, and Hope reached over and clasped Anne's hand. "We're in as much shock as you are." She patted her hand.

"Literally, I never, *like*, saw that coming." Kandi whipped eggs in a bowl.

Normally Anne would come back with a silly retort about Kandi's liberal use of *literally* or *like*, but she said nothing.

"How did you all hear that he'd been arrested? When did this happen? What was he arrested for? What evidence do they have?" The questions spilled from Anne's lips.

"Hold up there." Hope raised her palm up to stop Anne's barrage.

"Sorry." Anne ran her fingers through her hair and pulled it together before letting the messy curls drop back onto her shoulders.

As Kandi added butter to an omelet pan, Hope spun the account. "This morning, I was on my way over to the Inn with Kandi when Stewart showed up. He'd been in town getting some materials for a carpentry job over at Stanley's when he saw Deputy Ruiz pull up at the sheriff's office. He started to say hello when he noticed that there was another person in the backseat. It was Carson. Ruiz brought him out and Carson's hands were cuffed behind his back." She paused as Kandi asked if they wanted spinach and mushrooms in their omelets. Both Hope and Anne nodded yes.

"Stewart was shocked. He was going to go inside when he noticed Police Chief Everett in his cruiser. He went over and inquired about what he'd just seen." Hope paused her story as Kandi set down the warm omelets in front of the women. She pulled some croissants from a warming tray and set those on the table as well. After everything was on the table, Kandi refilled everyone's coffee cups and set tumblers of fresh-squeezed orange juice at their places.

Anne smiled up at the perky young woman. "Kandi, you are truly a treasure. You make things feel so much better." She took a bite of the fluffy omelet. "And your cooking is heavenly."

"Agreed." Hope speared some egg, mushroom, and spinach on her fork.

After everyone had eaten a few bites, Anne said, "Was Stewart able to get Chief Everett to say what had happened?"

"Yes, and no. He would never come out with the full story, so Stewart had to ask questions—Is this to do with the arson, for example—and figure out Everett's answers. Sad to see an officer of the law be on the wrong side of it.'"

"Why would Carson have anything to do with the fire at your place?" Anne set her fork down. "It makes no sense."

"I agree. But Spencer said the kid told him he was the sheriff, and Mama said it was the sheriff who took her away from the house."

Anne speared a piece of the omelet. "Yes, but your mom said that he was a young man. Carson isn't young."

Hope laughed. "In relation to who? You, me, my mom?"

"Oh, I guess you're right. But don't you think it's weird that he would have given out his name?" Anne set down her fork. "That makes absolutely no sense."

"What's, *like,* our next move?" Kandi chirped.

"I have no clue, Watson."

Hope shook her head. "Well, I do. Anne, you need to go to the source. You need to go see Carson."

Chapter Seventeen

The sheriff's office didn't look any different from the last time Anne had been inside. She walked in to find Thelma, the sheriff's elderly receptionist, squinting at a pile of papers in front of her. Another deputy sat a desk across from Thelma, typing something on a computer. Anne stole a glance to the two cells in the far left corner—one she knew held Sheriff Carson.

"I'm here to see Sheriff Carson."

"Are you now?" Thelma pushed her readers up and narrowed her eyes at Anne. "Reason?"

Anne wondered what she should say. "I'm a friend."

The deputy looked up from his paperwork and gave a nod of affirmation to Thelma. She pulled out a log and shoved her bony, wrinkled finger toward a line. "Sign here."

After Anne had left her purse with the deputy, he walked her to the back cell. Inside, Carson sat on a cot covered in a scratchy wool blanket. He looked over at her but made no move to get up. "I, I... heard, and I wanted to come and offer my help."

He jumped up from the cot and grabbed the bars. Anne jumped back. She quickly looked over her shoulder but neither Thelma nor the deputy had seen her reaction.

He spoke in low, angry tones. "No. I do not want your help. Stay out of it."

She lowered her voice to match his, as she knew Thelma would strain to hear every word.

"But you didn't do it."

"Didn't I?" He chuckled. "You think you know me so well, don't you?" His tone grew more menacing. "You don't know me. They got me all right. Fingerprints. Items to start the fires. Now they're even checking to see if I could have shot Ray Lawrence with my gun."

Anne recoiled. She couldn't be wrong about him. But she'd been wrong about others in the past. She'd trusted before and been conned.

"Okay, fine. Have it your way. I thought you were one of the good guys."

"You thought wrong."

Anne fought back anger and tears. "I see that now."

"Leave. I have nothing more to say to you." He sat back down on the cot.

Anne struggled to keep her composure as she gathered her purse from the deputy. She headed for the door, but Thelma's raspy voice stopped her. "You have to sign out too."

Anne rolled her eyes but walked over to the woman. A sheet of paper was next to her name. In a rough scribble, it said simply, "Don't listen to him."

Puzzled, Anne looked up to see that Thelma had cupped her chin with her arthritic hands but placed one finger over her lips. She glanced over toward the deputy who looked up at her.

"Need anything else?"

"No. no. Thank you." She set the pen down and locked eyes with Thelma.

The old women grabbed the book and shoved it into a desk drawer. "Now get on outta here. We don't have time for no loitering."

Anne put the crossbody bag over her shoulder. Outside, she waited for her eyes to adjust to the sunshine. While she was here, she might as well go see Hope's shop in daylight. As she turned, a figure jogged across the street and around a building.

It's that woman again. That's when bells went off. Last night, Anne had seen her standing across the street in the gathered crowd. Who was this woman and why had she come to Carolan Springs?

Chapter Eighteen

Anne had arrived back at the Inn to find Kandi and Spencer cleaning out the vacated rooms. They hauled the sheets and towels down to a large bin on the back porch for laundry pick-up. Then Spencer left to go work at Patty's Pet Shop for the afternoon.

"That's what he said?" Kandi's eyes had widened so much that she reminded Anne of an owl.

"Yes. Then Thelma's note. What did she mean about not listening to him?"

"Stewart told me that rumors are flying about Sheriff Carson being involved in the fires, Ray's death, even Bill's injury."

"Rumors are just that. Rumors. What would he have to gain from any of this?" Anne shook her head. "What's the connection for everything?"

"You mean, *like*, the motive?"

"Exactly. What would be his motive?"

"Maybe it was Bill."

Anne tipped her head. "Bill? Really? You don't usually try to kill yourself to frame someone else."

"Okay, maybe Cal Bennett came back early—or never left—found Ray in his greenhouse, so he killed him. Then he left town for an alibi."

"So, he burned down his own greenhouse, and almost his home, to cover up a murder in his greenhouse?"

Kandi twisted her mouth. "Yeah. I guess that doesn't make much sense. This is a tough one. It does seem that we don't have that many suspects and it all points to Sheriff Carson."

The door flew open and Kandi's brothers came in, back from their trip to Boulder. "Kandi," Kevin started. "We're out of here. This place has bad vibes." Karl nodded his head in agreement.

"Really? You haven't been here very long. Where to now?"

"We're catching a ride to the west coast and then taking a freighter over to Asia."

"But…" Kandi pouted.

"Hey, sis, we've got to live in the moment." Kevin hugged her.

"Truth, man. This place is too—" Karl joined in.

"Yeah, too."

Anne couldn't figure out what she was hearing other than the boys would be leaving.

After the boys left, Kandi spoke up. "I love my brothers but they're so…"

"Weird?" Anne laughed.

Kandi giggled. "I guess. I love my home. I don't see that it has any bad vibes other than—"

"Let's not go down that road."

"Okay. What road should we go down?"

"I think we need to go back and talk with the Connors. They may be able to shed some light on what we're missing."

"All right. Let's get this stuff finished up and we can see about going over there this afternoon or tomorrow."

Kandi emptied the dishwasher. "Oh, I saw that lady again."

"The one staying at Sam's?"

"Yes. She was on the trail at the back of the house. Probably out on a run."

"Probably." While it wasn't uncommon to see people from town, this woman seemed to be turning up quite a lot. Had she seen what happened at Hope's shop? Maybe they needed to ask her some questions.

Want to drive out to Sam's and see if we can catch her?" Anne wiped down the counters and loaded up the trash. Anne recalled how the woman had warned her in a similar way to Carson.

Kandi nodded. "Sounds like a good idea. Everything's done here for now and Hope will be over in a while to take over, so we could leave any time."

"Okay, my truck or yours?" Anne knew Kandi preferred driving and she didn't mind being the passenger.

"Mine. Meet you at my house in, *like*, fifteen?"

Anne opened the back door. "Let's say forty-five. I need to set up Mouser's food trays and I'd like to take a quick shower and change."

"K. See ya then. I'll honk, and you can come out."

"Great." She reached over and gave Kandi a quick kiss on the cheek. At home, Anne filled up Mouser's timed trays with dry food and some treats. She refilled his water and quickly checked the mail she'd picked up earlier. A cool shower helped to invigorate her and gave her time to think.

Carson has been charged. There's sufficient evidence to show his guilt so why don't I believe it? Then there's Thelma's note. Why didn't she just say it out loud to me? Who did she not want to hear—Carson or the deputy sitting nearby? Why the secrecy?

Anne turned off the water and began the process of drying her hair. Out loud she said, "What is the connection?"

She drew with her finger on the steamed mirror.

Bill and Lori—attack and vandalism.

Ray Lawrence-murdered.

Bennetts—greenhouse, fire, murder victim, house almost destroyed.

Hope's place—arson.

Nothing made any sense. Nothing connected.

Anne had finished getting ready when she heard Kandi's horn. She went out the back door, around the house and headed to the front. Climbing up on the truck's automatic step, she grabbed hold of the handle and pulled herself up into the cab.

The day was nice, and they let the windows down to enjoy the breeze. One great thing about Colorado was the low humidity, which allowed such a treat. They pulled up at Sam's and as they watched, Mary came out on the porch. The woman wore a tank top and shorts, sweat glistening on her arms and face.

"Hi, there!" She waved at the pair.

"Hello. Hope we're not intruding. We just thought we'd come over and see how you're doing."

"Thanks." She wiped her face with the back of her arm. "Sam had called and asked if I needed anything and I asked if I could use his gym—so I've been working out."

Kandi responded, "Well, it's working, you're totally, *like*, buff."

"I need it in my line of work."

"What's that?" Anne inquired, shielding her eyes from the sun.

"You want to come in and have a drink?" Mary replied, ignoring Anne's question.

"We don't want to bother you if you're in the middle of working out."

"Nah. It's a good time for a break anyway." She led them into the house. Anne turned and looked out over the lake, sparkling against the sun's reflection.

"I've always been envious of Sam's place. It's so nice."

"I have to agree with you there. Beer? Soda? Water?" Mary pulled bottles from the fridge.

"I'll take a beer." Anne reached over to take a bottle of Bristol's Beehive Honey Wheat from her hand.

"Soda for me." Kandi took the offering.

Mary grabbed a beer and closed the refrigerator. "Want to sit out on the deck?"

Anne and Kandi nodded agreement. "Yes."

After they'd all settled into deck chairs and admired the lake view again, Mary said, "So what do I owe the pleasure of your company? You're obviously here for a purpose, not a simple side trip way out into the woods."

Anne wiped the sweat off her bottle. "You're right. We hate to bother you, but to be honest, some crazy happenings have been going on and we thought you might be able to help us."

Mary took a deep swig of her beer before replying. "In what way? I don't see how I could help you with anything. I'm not from here."

Kandi set her soda down on the table between her and Anne's chairs. "Here's the deal. We have a friend who's been arrested for something he didn't do."

Mary looked between them. "A friend?"

"Sheriff Carson." Anne held the beer between both hands, the cold felt good in her grip.

"The sheriff? He's been arrested? For what?"

She's turning the tables on us. We're supposed to be asking the questions and not the ones giving the answers.

"Supposedly arson. Of my friend's shop. I think you saw it the other evening." Anne sought to flip the narrative.

Mary smiled. "Yes. I'd gone out to dinner in town and was strolling the main street that evening when I heard the sirens."

"You weren't there before it happened? You didn't see anyone—a young man, running away from the scene? Anything that could be helpful." Anne set her drink next to Kandi's.

"Sorry, no. I was a few blocks down doing some window shopping when I heard the commotion."

"Shoot!" Kandi crossed her arms. "Another dead end."

"I have to ask—why are you involved in this? Shouldn't you let the police handle it? They know what they're doing."

Anne retorted, "If they knew what they were doing they never would have arrested Carson."

"Carson?"

"I mean, Sheriff Carson." Anne reached for her drink.

"Do you think you may be a bit too close to it to be unbiased?" the woman asked Anne.

Anne's cheeks flushed. "I don't know..."

"That's what I thought." Mary pulled a tan, muscled leg up with her arm and stretched. "You'd be surprised how many people want to believe someone's innocent." She repeated the gesture with the other leg.

"But he is innocent." Kandi crossed her arms in defiance.

Mary smiled at her. "You want that to be true. But it doesn't mean it is."

"How do you know that?"

"I just know."

Standoff. Anne knew they wouldn't get anywhere with this type of back and forth. "We appreciate your taking the time to speak with us. We're just trying to help a friend." Anne stood, and Kandi grabbed her soda.

Mary also stood up and twisted her back in a stretch. "I will say this. Stay out of it. You, or someone you love, could get hurt."

"That's what Car—" Kandi burst out.

Anne touched Kandi on the arm to silence her. "We have to do what we can."

Mary responded, "Then do so without making yourself known."

What did that mean?

"Oh, I forgot. Sam is supposed to be back tomorrow, and I think I'll stay on for a few more days. Do you have a room available at the Inn?"

"Yes," Kandi affirmed. "We had a group leave today. I'll hold you a room for tomorrow and you can, *like,* let me know when you think you might check out when you register."

"Great." They'd headed down to the truck when they heard another vehicle approaching. A black pickup came slowly up the drive, tires crunching on the gravel. It pulled over toward a copse of trees and as the woman watched, a young man exited the vehicle.

Deputy Ruiz.

He raised his hand in greeting and walked over to the group.

"Deputy." Anne shielded her eyes with her hand.

"I'm off duty. You can call me Benjamin or Ruiz." He adjusted the blue baseball cap he wore.

"Did you come out to see Mary?"

"Um, no. Nice to meet you." Deputy Ruiz shook hands with Mary.

Even with the pretense, Anne felt like they'd met before. Maybe her imagination was on overdrive.

"Nice to meet you," Mary responded to Ruiz.

"Then what are you, *like*, doing out here? Sam's out with the scouts until tomorrow." Kandi cocked her head, a habit that Anne had become endeared to seeing.

"Sam lets me park my truck here, as it's easier to access the lake through his property. I've got my fishing gear in the truck."

Anne smiled at him. "That's great." She turned to Kandi. "Ready?"

"Bye." Kandi pulled her keys out and walked over to the truck. As they got in, Anne watched as Ruiz pulled out a tackle box and retractable pole from the truck's bumper storage. He waved, and Kandi began her three-point turn. As they drove down the road, Anne looked into the rearview side mirror.

Mary had joined Deputy Ruiz and they stood watching the truck drive away.

Was Deputy Ruiz really there to fish? Why had he acted like he didn't know the woman but seemed like he really did? Maybe they were starting to see one another—they were both around the same age—late twenties looked like, and very fit. Could it be they just didn't want others to know they were seeing each other?

Then words came spilling back in her mind. Mary had tried to deter them from helping Carson. She'd almost implied that Carson could be guilty. That people could be wrong about someone they know. Or at least think they know. What about Deputy Ruiz? Of all the people in town, he had the ability to frame Carson the easiest. He'd been first on the scene to find the Bennett's place in flames. He'd have the same type of weapon that Carson used. Plus, he hadn't been in the town that long before all the bad stuff started happening. Was Deputy Ruiz involved in something to get rid of Sheriff Carson? Maybe that was why Thelma hadn't spoken. She knew it might get back to Ruiz. She had to go to someone with her suspicions. But who?

"Kandi, we need to take a detour. Take me to the police station. I need to talk to Chief Everett."

Chapter Nineteen

When they arrived at the police station, Everett was out but Officer Dale was on duty. He led them into a conference room, grabbed a yellow pad and followed the pair inside.

After recounting their concerns, Dale thanked them and reiterated what everyone else had said—basically, stay out of it so no one gets hurt. Let the police handle it. He couldn't promise that he could do anything as far as Carson was concerned, since that was a different agency altogether. But he'd fill Chief Everett in on their suspicions concerning Ruiz.

After exiting the police station, they stopped in at the herbal shop where Stewart, with Spencer's help, was pulling out the destroyed walls and installing new two-by-sixes.

"Looks like you guys are making some good progress."

"Spence here has been a huge help."

Anne smiled. The young man had blossomed since Stewart had taken an interest in him. No longer his sullen self, his quick wit and work ethic had made him an essential part of the Inn's success.

"I hope it's, like, you know, okay for me to be helping out here instead of at the Inn today." He pushed his hair off his face.

"Very acceptable. This is the priority right now. Thanks for being such a help to us." Anne patted him on the shoulder.

Spencer beamed.

"You guys are really working hard. Want to stop by tonight for a BBQ?" Kandi quipped.

"Yes!" Stewart and Spencer responded.

"Great. Seven, seven-thirty work?"

"We'll be there." Stewart picked up a hammer and went back to work.

Outside, they got back in the truck and Anne turned to face Kandi. "Are you ever going to give that young man a real chance?"

"Who says I haven't?" Kandi made a face.

Laughing, Anne said, "Okay. Good. Now, let's go out to the Connors. I called Lori this morning and she said that Bill is up for visitors."

The drive was nice and soon they were seated outside in the shade of a copse of blue spruce.

Once settled in, Anne queried, "Bill, how's the head?"

"Better," he replied. "The headaches aren't as frequent, and I always wondered what I'd look like in a buzz cut." He rubbed his hand on the side of his head not covered in a bandage. "Pretty easy and nice for summer. I may keep it."

Lori rolled her eyes and groaned but everyone laughed.

"What do you think happened?"

Bill sat back, stretched his legs out in front and clasped his hands together. He looked over at Lori.

"It was vandalism. Pure and simple. I just came in and they panicked."

Anne knew she was being given a rehearsed answer. No questioning. No reasoning.

"Why do you think someone came all the way out here?"

"Lori told me you found the pot plants."

Anne shook her head in the affirmative but said nothing.

"It's really expensive if you need to take it on a daily basis and we were trying juicing and also having the plant being made into oil. I'd been buying it elsewhere and figured I'd start growing our own. I have space in the greenhouse."

"Where were you getting the plants?"

"From Cal Bennett."

Cal Bennett? That was one connection.

He shook his head. "I don't know where I'll get plants to replace the damaged ones. Thankfully," he patted Lori's hand, "we still had enough cannabinoid oil and salve, so we were able to keep Lori's pain in check while I was in the hospital."

"The Bennetts were growing weed? Wow, *like*, they seemed so, *like*, normal."

Bill chuckled. "They are normal. You'd probably be surprised how many people 'partake' in this town."

"But that doesn't answer the question of why someone came out here and attacked you."

"Kids. I think someone must have found out that I had pot plants and they came out to grab the buds."

"I wouldn't think kids would even know what to take."

"Possibly." He crossed his legs.

"But someone tried to kill you."

Bill shook his head then thought better of it. He reached his hand up to the bandage. "I think they got scared. I don't think they wanted to hurt me. Just get me out of the way so I couldn't see who they were and report them."

"But Lori said you were getting a gun."

He looked over at Lori who focused on her hands in her lap.

"Well, you can never be too careful."

Lori diverted the conversation and Anne got the hint. They bid the couple goodbye and headed back to the bed and breakfast. In the office, Anne found Hope going over paperwork.

"How's it going?"

Hope looked up with a smile on her face. "I think we've actually entered into the profit side of things."

Kandi had followed Anne into the office and raised her hands into the air, doing a combination of hopping and dancing in a circle. "We're going to be rich." We're going to be—"

Hope wadded up a piece of paper and threw it at her. "You're already rich, you goof."

Anne looked over at the innocent looking young woman who giggled. "I'm gonna be richer."

No one would guess that Kandi was a millionaire due to an inheritance left by her dead mother. She lived in the same house and was the same sweet but ditsy young woman that Anne loved as much as she would her own daughter.

"Hello?" A woman's voice interrupted.

Anne moved toward the hall that led to the kitchen. Mary stood there.

"I wondered if my room might be ready." She was dressed in black jeans and a black tee-shirt. Her hair pushed back into a tight bun. No makeup. No jewelry.

That woman is all business, thought Anne. She pointed toward the front where the stairs leading to the upper floors were located. "I can take you. Follow me."

"Great." The woman picked up her small black roller-bag.

When Anne had settled Mary in her room, she returned to find Stewart down in the kitchen. Kandi was mixing something in a bowl that looked to be the makings for cupcakes.

"Hey, Stewart? How's everything in your world?"

He pulled up a chair and sat down. "Good, though I'm a bit disappointed."

"Oh, about what? Kandi turn down your proposal again?"

His face turned beet-red and Kandi shot Anne a look of frustration.

Anne went over and squeezed Stewart's shoulder. "Sorry. I was teasing, and it came out badly."

"It's okay." The color was already leaving his face. He scratched the day-old beard he wore. "No, it's the Bennett place."

"Soda? Iced Tea?" Anne held up a jar of sun tea.

"Tea, please. Does it have sugar?"

"No." Anne set it down on the counter and started retrieving glasses from a cabinet.

"Oh, man, I got to have sweet tea." He turned in his chair. "Kandi, you got any sugar over there?"

Anne bit her lip so as to not embarrass the two young people again with another of her obvious match-making quips.

"I've got sugar or honey."

Hope had finished her work and had joined the pair. "I'll take honey for mine. Thanks." She'd just sat down when the back door swung open. It was Sam, browned and looking healthy after his camping trip.

"Sam!" Kandi bounced over and gave him a hug.

"Hey, girl." He ruffled her head not unlike he would do his dog, Hank.

The pair had connected and now they were like an older brother and younger sister.

"Tea?"

"I was just stopping by—"

"I hope I'm not intruding." Mary stood in the door.

Hope waved her in. "Certainly not. Please, join us. We're just having some tea."

"Is it sweetened?"

"No." Anne replied.

"Oh good, I hate sweet tea."

As she and Stewart argued the merits of sweetened and unsweetened tea, Anne spied that Sam's focus was clearly on Mary. The young woman had changed out of other clothing and now wore a tank top covered by another top and a pair of shorts. Her legs, like Sam's, were brown from being out in the sun and were as muscled as her upper arms.

Anne realized she was pouting with a little bit of jealousy over Sam's obvious infatuation with the woman.

Argh. You don't want him when he wants you. Now you want him because he's interested in someone else? Make up your mind, woman.

The woman quickly downed the tea. I'm out for a run. I heard there's a trail close to the house I can take?"

"Yes. I can show you." Hope stood.

"Don't worry, Hope. I'll show her." Sam smiled at the woman and she smiled back.

Then Anne remembered Ruiz being out at Sam's. It didn't look like he'd come to fish but more like he was visiting her. One thing Anne did know was that she didn't want Sam to get hurt. "Oh, Sam?" She stopped the pair as they made their way to the door.

He turned back. "Yes?"

"We saw Ruiz over at your place the other day."

A swift glimmer of emotion passed over the woman's face. Anne wondered if she'd opened up a relationship the woman wanted to be kept secret.

"Yeah. He sometimes goes out there to go fishing."

The woman visibly relaxed. "Ready?"

After the pair had left the house, everyone turned back to Anne. "What?"

"Always on the lookout for clues, huh, Ms. Marple?" Hope replied.

"I hope you don't consider me as old as Ms. Marple, and I don't knit, so…"

Hope laughed. "Anyway, what was the point of all the questioning?"

"When Kandi and I went out to Sam's to visit Mary, Ruiz showed up."

"That is interesting. I know that I caught them talking to each other after my shop was damaged."

"You did?"

"Yes. After I went over to the ambulance to stay with Mom, I saw that she was standing over by a tree. They were talking but very quietly. I thought it was strange at the time but then I figured I was in some shock, so I didn't think to say anything about it."

"Where would they have even met? Did she know him before coming to the Springs or meet here?"

Kandi sat down next to Stewart. "Maybe he went out to Sam's before and they met then."

"I guess, but they acted like they didn't know each other when we were out there."

"Hmm, that's true. Maybe, they wanted to keep it on the, you know, the down-low." Kandi sipped her sweetened tea.

"I guess, but really, what difference does it make to anything? Just trying to figure out if there's anything that can help us get Carson out of jail."

Hope clasped her hands around the glass. "I expect he'll be out today sometime."

"Really? Why's that?" Anne poured some more tea and drizzled a bit of honey in it.

"I told them I wasn't going to press charges."

"What? Why?"

"Because I know he didn't do it."

"You don't know. He even told me himself that I didn't know him."

"Okay, we'll have to agree to disagree." Hope laughed.

"What's so funny?"

"You are, you nit." Hope shook her head. "Quit trying to push the best thing that could happen to you away."

Kandi started and turned to Hope. "What? Are you talking to me?"

Hope sighed. "No. I was talking to Anne. And yes, to you too. Oh, forget it. Stewart, you were going to tell us something before everything went haywire. What was it?"

Stewart held up his glass as Kandi poured him more tea. He added three heaping teaspoons of sugar to it. "Not sure what I was saying,"

"You were disappointed about something," Anne replied.

"Oh, yeah. That." He ran his hands through his hair. "I figured that the Bennett job would offer a lot of us in town work, but they've brought their own crews in."

"That is a bit strange but not unheard of, I guess."

"I went out to see if they had any work and they've got lots of RV's parked around where the guys sleep. It just seems really strange."

Anne emptied her glass. "What did they say when you talked to them?"

"I never even got a chance. They've fenced it in, and they were putting up a gate, so I couldn't drive onto the property."

"Not surprising. If it's going to be a big event center, they'll need to keep people from coming in when it's not open." Hope stretched her back and changed positions in her chair.

"I guess. I don't know. Just seems weird." He rubbed his beard again. "I was eating dinner at the new hamburger place on Poplar when a group of them came in. They sat in the booth behind me, so it wasn't like I couldn't hear what they were saying."

"What did they, *like*, say?" Kandi rested her head on her hand and looked up at Stewart.

"What?" he gulped.

"What were the guys saying?" Anne grew frustrated.

"Oh, they weren't happy about having to sign an NDA."

Kandi bobbed her head. "A what?"

He turned to her. "A non-disclosure agreement. One of the guys said it's the first time he's ever signed such a thing."

"Well, I can probably understand it. One of those guys goes out into the community and says what they are building, and it kills the marketing buzz." Hope stood up and took her glass over to the dishwasher.

Anne also stood. "That does make sense." She looked out the window and caught a glimpse of Sam coming back up from the trail. Had they been talking for that long?

"I'm going home. In case anyone needs me—that's where I plan to be for a while."

She hugged Kandi and kissed her forehead. She shook Stewart's outreached hand before grabbing him up in a hug too. Hope came over and they were hugging when Sam came inside.

"Is this a hug-fest? Can I get in on that?"

"Sure." Anne and Hope both gave him a hug.

"Later." Anne waved at the group and enjoyed the short walk back to her house. She checked Mouser's food and water and kicked off her shoes. She was dozing when the doorbell rang.

Who could that be?

Chapter Twenty

Officer Dale stood in the doorway.

"Officer Dale, hello. Can I help you?"

"Ms. Freemont. You were very helpful in giving us information before and I wanted to stop by and see if there was anything else you wanted to share that might help."

"In what way?"

"As you probably know, Ms. Boswell has said she won't be pressing charges."

"Yes, she told me that. I don't understand it but that's her decision, not mine."

"I think people want to believe the best of others, even when it's not true."

"You're right." Anne stepped back from the door. "Did you want to come in?" She stifled a yawn.

"No. Thank you. We're just continuing to look into the fire at your friend's shop and also the attack over at Bill's. I heard they released him from the hospital."

"Yes. He's doing better. But..." Anne decided not to say anything about Bill's decision to buy a gun.

"I hate to bother him. First, his wife's cancer. Then the attack. It's a lot for them."

Anne nodded her head in agreement.

"Did he see anyone, hear anything that could help us find who did this?"

"No. He thinks it was kids and that the attack wasn't planned."

"Good. Good to know. That's helpful. Anything else?"

"Do you know what's going on at the Bennett place?"

He looked down at her, but his sunglasses obscured his eyes. "Like what? Why do you ask?"

"Stewart was just saying they are making the workers sign an NDA and now they're putting up a gate. Seems fast for all this to happen right after the fire and the... "

"Yes, it was horrible about Ray Lawrence, but you know he was in with bad company. I've seen it happen before. People think they can make an easy buck and they don't know how entangled they can get with criminals."

Anne nodded her head. "Spencer told us that Ray was always trying to sell pot to the foster kids and at the high school."

"Sad, isn't it?" He stuck his thumbs in his gear belt. "You try to put people on the straight and narrow, but sometimes you can't help them. Then someone gets it in their head to get justice."

"You mean, like, a vigilante?"

"Well, it's not my place to say, but think about it." He ticked a list off his fingers. "Ray Lawrence—sold pot to kids, the Bennetts—pot growers, Bill Connor—pot in his greenhouse." He shrugged.

The idea of a vigilante against drugs hadn't occurred to Anne before. Maybe that was the thread that tied everything together. But who would...? She gasped.

"Yes. I see you've got there. Who would think they're doing the world a favor by getting rid of—"

"But he could just arrest them."

Officer Dale shook his head. "Unless he had caught Ray in the act of selling to minors—no proof."

"I don't know. Lori's his cousin and I can't see him hitting Bill over the head."

"Maybe he thought it would cause a divide in the family? Maybe it was an accident?"

"I don't see how it could have been an accident. Plus, being against drugs doesn't mean you'll burn down someone's house and kill somebody." She crossed her arms.

"Again, this is all supposition on my part. Ray could have just been at the wrong place at the wrong time. The coroner said he had drugs in his system when he died, so maybe he fell asleep in the greenhouse and whoever torched it didn't know he was in there."

"Yes, that's plausible." Anne nodded in agreement. "But hadn't he been shot?"

"How do you know so much?"

Anne ignored Officer Dale's question. "What about Hope's shop? Hope doesn't sell pot. In fact, she's said she'll never include it as she doesn't know it enough to feel that she can prescribe it medicinally."

"Could be a mistake. Could be to scare her—or you—off."

"Scare us off?"

"The rumor mill says you all like to play private detective." He crossed his arms and his shirt strained against his arm muscles.

"Only when I have no other choice. We were just talking about how nothing makes sense. This one looks like we won't be able to help the police."

"I like to hear you want to help the police. But with information only. It's our job to keep you safe and to find the bad guy. Anyway, if you think of anything… no matter how insignificant, you call me." He tipped his fingers to his glasses and headed down the steps. "Oh." He turned around. "Carson is being released. You be careful."

A week of calm came after Officer Dale's visit and Anne was looking forward to the next week's activities. They'd set up another beehive visit with Bill after he assured her he had enough help to show honey extraction. The guests for that tour would also get to take home a jar of honey. Even people from the town and the state who were not staying at the bed and breakfast had signed up for it. The bed and breakfast was continually full of people arriving even before others left. Often, Anne would hear laughter through her open windows, and it made her smile.

Ralph's old house—rest his soul—seemed to have put aside its past bad experiences and now thrived with life. Anne smiled as she hummed a tune. A warm and gentle breeze floated inside as she opened her upstairs bedroom window. She spotted Sam's truck next door. He seemed to spend quite a lot of time over there with Mary lately. When Anne had gone over to help Kandi with breakfast in the morning, Sam and Mary would often be stretching and gearing up for a run. Anne desperately hoped that Mary wasn't stringing both Sam and Ruiz along for a short ride during her visit.

Anne spoke aloud, "Quit being a mom. He's an adult." That's when the dots connected. She liked Sam but more like a son or a friend than anything more. Maybe this was the confirmation she needed to forget that part of her life.

She pulled the top sheet from the dresser and waved it over the bed. The doorbell rang.

"Not now," Anne muttered. It better not be some solicitor.

Anne let the sheet fall and then jumbled it up onto the bed.

She had made it halfway down the stairs when the bell rang again. "I'm coming!"

She threw open the front door, ready to send the caller packing.

It was Carson.

It still startled Anne when she saw him out of his normal sheriff's uniform. Today he wore a navy blue tee-shirt and a pair of blue cargo shorts. On his feet, he wore the ubiquitous pair of REI hiking boots seen on many people around Colorado. Even after his stint in jail, he still looked healthy and sported a golden tan.

"Anne."

"Oh, we're back on first names? Or at least my first name, not yours."

"You're right. My apologies. Ms. Freemont."

Anne huffed and crossed her arms. That man. Why wouldn't he just tell her his first name?

"Yes, Sheriff Carson?"

"I'm on leave pending further investigation so we can leave off the sheriff part for now." He made a motion with his hand. "Can I come in?"

She nodded yes and as she closed the door, she noticed Mary crossing the street. Anne waved, but the woman appeared not to notice her.

What's up with her? I know she saw us.

She motioned for Carson to sit in a large overstuffed chair across from the sofa. When he didn't take a seat, she plopped down on the sofa. "Okay. I'm all ears. What's up?"

He sat down opposite her on the couch, which gave her a start. He appeared contrite when he said, "I know you're going to give me a hard time on this—"

"I don't—"

He held his hand up to silence her. "Yes, you do. But that's another story. As much as I hate to say this, I need your help."

Anne wanted to gloat, to react in ways that were payback for all the times he'd made jokes at her expense. Instead, she simply replied, "How?"

Carson took a deep breath. "Thank you."

"Something to drink?"

"No. I— well, as you know, they arrested me in connection with Hope's arson. I didn't do it."

"Why did you act like you did to me in the jail?"

"I wanted you to back off. I didn't know who I could trust, and I didn't want you, Hope, or Kandi getting hurt."

"You mean Ruiz?"

Carson sat up. "What makes you say that? Do you know something?"

"I know he's the one that arrested you."

"He was doing his duty. Although, technically it was Sam."

Anne made a face. "Sam? What do you mean?"

"The coroner is the only one who has the power to arrest the sheriff. He's acting coroner until the next election when Doc Reynolds retires. Ruiz was there but under Sam's orders."

"Okay, whoever arrested you, Hope is not pressing charges, so it should be good now."

"It's not that easy. I'm being told that other charges may be pending. Serious charges."

"You mean like Ray's death?"

"Yes. Possibly looking at manslaughter from what I'm hearing."

"How do you know that?"

He zipped his lips. "Can't reveal my sources."

"I'll bet one of your sources has permed gray hair." Anne laughed. "Okay, so what do you need my help with?"

"I can't sit around waiting for others to seal my fate without a fight. However, if they do think I'm doing that, then they'll be less inclined to keep me in their sights."

"Who's they?" Anne leaned closer.

"I don't know. But I've been listening to anything and everything around town. I also spoke with Stewart."

"About the Bennett place?"

"Not exactly. He told me that he overheard some guys talking down at the Hall about El Toro."

"El Toro? Doesn't that mean the bull?"

"Yes. That name is popping up a lot lately."

"Do you think it's the cartel?" Anne shivered. "Here, in Carolan Springs?"

He shook his head. "I don't know. But something's going on and they're trying to keep me out of the way."

"That's really scary," Anne commented.

"I know. That's why I didn't—I still don't—want you involved." He stood up and jammed his hands in his pockets. "But I need a cover, and you would make a good one. Plus, I know you won't stop meddling."

Anne sprang up from the couch. "That's—"

"True?"

She sighed and shrugged her shoulders. "Okay, possibly. What do you need from me?"

"Remember the opening of the B-n-B?"

Anne nodded. How could she ever forget that kiss?

"We need to put on an act again. And make it good."

"Meaning?"

"Dating. Us. You and me."

Anne laughed, "What?"

He shoved his hands in his pockets. "In some ways, I'm worried it could make you more of a target. In other ways, I think it could keep you safer. I've just got to take that chance."

Anne realized he was speaking more to himself than to her.

"Well, that's probably the most unromantic date request I've ever had."

He stopped and put his hands on her upper arms. "I'm serious, Anne. This is—could be—a deadly proposition. Are you willing to take the risk?"

A shiver went down Anne's spine. For the first time since she'd known him, she saw fear in Carson's eyes.

She gulped. "Yes."

He let go of her arms. Sighing, he pointed to the back. "Bathroom?"

"It's being worked on, but you can use the bath upstairs. What's your plan?"

"First, we need to go out around town, let people see us. Maybe dinner out tonight?"

She nodded. "I can do that. Here, let me show you where the bathroom is."

They walked up the stairs in silence and after Carson went toward the end of the hall, Anne returned to her room. She picked up a pillow that had fallen on the floor and stuffed it into a crisp, clean pillowcase. She had just finished the other one and turned back to the sheets when Carson appeared in the doorway.

Chapter Twenty-One

"Here, let me help you with that."

"You better watch out. Those are the best words women want to hear from a man."

He laughed. "Yes, my wife always said she lucked out with me over all those 'other' bum husbands."

Anne swept her hand under the mattress, tucking in the sheet. "I'm really sorry about your wife."

"Thanks. When you say, 'til death do us part,' you don't ever think that it will happen so soon."

"And you never remarried?"

"No. I didn't think I could handle any more heartache if anything happened again."

"Yes." Anne knew exactly how heartache could stop you loving or trusting again.

Carson grabbed the coverlet for the bed, and with one swift motion, he covered the bed. He smoothed it up over the pillow and then along the side.

"It looks like you've done this a time or two."

"You forget, I've been on my own a while. And I have my own house."

She nodded, and they headed out from the bedroom to the hallway. A meow greeted them.

Carson reached down and picked up the cat. "Why, Mouser, how big you've grown and what a handsome man you are." He stroked the cat's fur, and Mouser began purring loudly.

He set Mouser down, who then wrapped around Carson's bare legs a couple of turns and bounded off down the stairs.

"Does that mean what I think it means?" He smiled down at her.

"Yes, yes it does. He wants food."

They broke down laughing and walked in companionable silence down the stairs.

"Where would you like to go this evening?"

"Oh." Anne had forgotten. "How about you choose? Where do you think would be the best place to start the rumor mill?"

"Good point. How about the Hall? It's casual and all you have to do is get those old codgers to talk to their wives, and bam, we're in business."

"Sounds good. Say seven?"

"How about five-thirty?"

"Five-thirty!"

"Remember, these guys eat early, or they have to get home for dinner. That may even be late."

Anne sighed. "Oh, okay."

"One more thing before I go."

"Yes?"

He came and stood in front of her, close but not touching. She stared up into dark brown eyes.

"I'll be putting on a lot of PDA, but not in a sleazy way."

"Okay, sure." She had a hard time concentrating.

"May I?"

She nodded.

He kissed her.

Then she kissed him.

Then he kissed her.

"Oh, stop it. It's not a competition." They laughed and kissed one more time.

"Thank you."

She wanted to scream out 'no—thank you' but she simply nodded her head. After they pulled apart from their embrace, she put her hand to her mouth. Years. Years since a man had kissed her like that.

"I don't know what I would have done if you would have said no on helping me out."

Her mouth dropped open. Was this just a ruse they were playing?

As if he had read her mind, he reached over and clasped her chin. "You know I'm not playing with you."

Tears sprung to her eyes.

"Oh, I'm sorry. I didn't know you would take it like that." He pulled her into a hug.

"I'm o…kay," she stuttered, but before she could help it, the tears were flowing. He held her while she wept. When he released her, she looked up at him. "I——don't know why you're crying. I may have been without a woman in my life for a while, but it doesn't mean I don't know women." He softly kissed the top of her head. "Until tonight."

"More like this afternoon." She led him to the front door. After he left, she thought long and hard. Either she believed Carson, or she didn't. Could she think he was guilty of doing anything like starting a fire in Hope's shop or worse, being a killer vigilante? She concluded that she had to trust her gut. In her heart, he was a good man. Love may be blind, but she had to trust that she could still see and think clearly.

The evening turned out to be lots of fun. They enjoyed chicken-fried steak, mashed potatoes, green beans, and a house salad. Afterward, they chose to skip dessert and walk around Main Street. They took their time, walking hand in hand, stopping and looking in shop windows. From that vantage view, they enjoyed the spectacle mirrored in the windows of the people behind them staring, pointing and whispering behind their backs.

"We don't need to worry. I think we accomplished what we set out to do."

"Agreed. I wouldn't be surprised to see it as the headline on the Carolan Springs paper."

He turned to her. "I could get used to this type of detecting work."

"See, I told you that you needed me."

"And you were right." He stopped, and Anne realized that he may not have meant to say those words aloud. But there they were.

She couldn't help it. "I'm always right."

"Always?"

"Okay, ninety-eight percent of the time." She laughed and crooked her arm through his. They decided to stop at the new Italian restaurant for dessert. Anne ordered tiramisu and a coffee, while Carson went for the panna cotta with an espresso. The Hall had cleared out from the early birds and was now filling up with the younger crowd who came for local bands and dancing.

"Dance?" He motioned toward the Hall.

"Not tonight. Thanks."

"Okay, well as much as I hate to, I need to take you home."

They reached his car and Anne gasped. The tires had been slashed and his car keyed. His windows had also been smashed. As Carson surveyed the damage, they saw Officer Dale's cruiser pull up.

Anne called out, "Officer Dale! Over here!"

He got out of his car and came over to the pair. "Whoa, someone did a number on your vehicle."

"How do you know it's his vehicle?"

"I put in the license number when I pulled up."

"Oh, okay." That made sense.

"I got a call that someone heard a disturbance, so I came over."

"Did anyone see anything?"

Carson finally spoke. "Whoever did this knew the time to pick. Once the music starts up, there are so many people coming and going that people don't pay attention. A short amount of time when there's no one around and you can smash windows quickly."

Anne had gone around to the driver's side. She gasped. "Look at this."

The men came over and looked at letters scratched in the door. 'El Toro.'

"The bull." Anne's eyes grew wide.

"What do you make of that, Carson?" Officer Dale asked. He'd wiped the back of his neck as they talked, and his hand came back sweaty.

"No idea. Kids maybe?"

"We have been having lots of vandalism. You don't suppose—wait, another thought just came to me. Did you do this?" He faced Carson squarely.

Anne could see Carson getting angry, but he said nothing. She reached over and wrapped her hands around his tightened fist. His grip relaxed, and he held her hand. "No. I did not do this."

"I had to ask. You know, you could have been trying to divert suspicion away from yourself by having a vandal attack your car."

"While that could be a consideration to review," Carson said, reverting to his formal sheriff mode, "I wouldn't destroy my car to do so."

"All right. Let me get the particulars and I'll go ask if anyone saw or heard anything."

"Can I call a tow truck?"

Officer Dale nodded. If we need pictures, we can get them from you. I know you know the protocol."

He strode off to the Hall.

"I'm so sorry. Who could have done this? And why?"

"I don't know but I do know something he said was important."

"Yes? What?"

"About having someone do it. I need to talk to Spencer."

After the tow truck arrived, Kandi had arrived with Stewart to pick up the pair.

"Whoa, *like*, what happened?" Kandi ran over and hugged Anne.

"We're okay, sweetie. Someone with nothing better to do than destroy someone else's property."

Stewart came over and shook Carson's hand. The men watched as the vehicle was loaded onto the tow truck bed. "Any witnesses?"

"No. At least that are talking now."

"And no cameras here. The good thing about living in a small town… and the bad." Stewart nodded over to the women. "We'll take Anne home and then we can swing by your place. Do you need a vehicle? I can probably see about borrowing one for you."

"I'm good. I'll ride my bike into the shop tomorrow and find out how long it will take for the car to be fixed so I'll know how long to rent one. I've got my Jeep four-runner so I can use it for now."

"Too bad you can't use the cruiser."

"Yes, but I'm off duty until further notice."

Stewart reached up and stroked his facial hair. "I know they'll get everything cleared up."

"Maybe. Maybe not. Right now, I'm more concerned with that peach fuzz on your face."

"I'm thinking of growing a beard."

Carson slapped Stewart on the back. "Well, if you want me to show you how it's done, let me know."

Anne and Kandi joined them, and they headed over to Carson's house. He exited the truck and then turned back to Anne. He kissed her hand and said, "I'll see you at five."

"Five? For another early dinner tomorrow?"

"No, tomorrow morning. We're going hiking."

Chapter Twenty-Two

Anne dragged herself out of bed and climbed into a tank top, overshirt and hiking pants. Last night she packed a small backpack with her water, snacks, a hat, and windbreaker for the occasional mountain shower. She was lacing up her hiking boots when she heard a knock on the back door.

"Have you been waiting out here long? You could have rung the front doorbell."

"I didn't want to give people the wrong impression by seeing me on your front porch at five in the morning."

"Thanks for protecting my honor."

"'To serve and protect.' That's my motto."

"How about a motto of not getting up at the crack of dawn to go hiking? You know I love you but—"

"You love me?"

"It's a turn of phrase." She batted at him. "Which you know. Now, I can't handle all this early morning banter. Please tell me why you feel this need to go out where no one can see us. How does this help our progress on learning anything?"

"You'll see soon enough, ND." He watched as she pulled her hair up into a ponytail and stuck it through a baseball cap.

She saw him staring. "What?"

"Nothing. I tell you what. How about afterward we head over to Denver and eat breakfast at Snooze?

"Okay, you've redeemed yourself."

Patches of light mixed with the dark as they made their way along the first part of the trail. They spoke little, just enjoyed the birdsong or the occasional chipmunk that crossed their path. Anne noticed that Carson wasn't rushing, but he wasn't taking his time either.

"We're going somewhere. You have a purpose for this."

"I knew you were a smart woman the minute I met you." He smiled back at her and reached for her hand. As he did, he turned off the trail and headed up an embankment.

"We should really stay on the trail. What if we get lost?"

"Don't worry. I've lived in these mountains for many years. I have my GPS and I was a scout and have my compass. Plus, we're not going far. You'll see. Just listen to me and do exactly as I say it when I say it."

She nodded.

They hiked higher and higher until they came to a ridge. They went down into a smaller gulley and began another ascent.

"When I tell you, I need you to drop down. Got it?"

She nodded.

They were a few yards from the top of the ridge when he motioned for her to get down. She dropped to her belly and began scooting forward like a crab.

He laughed. "I didn't mean you had to turn into a commando. Just stay down low and close to trees."

He crouched down and began inching his way up the steep hill. As they both reached the top, Anne noticed from their vantage point they could see down onto the Bennett's old place. RV doors were opening and shutting, and the sound of men's voices was heard on the air.

Carson pulled out a set of binoculars from his pants pocket. He trained them down on the compound, now coming alive with workers.

"Tell me what you see." He handed the binoculars to Anne.

"Obviously, lots of men in all stages of dress. Ohhhhh—"

"Give me those back." He reached toward her.

She ignored him and moved the glasses away from the RVs and toward where a large building was going up. The building had metal studs and some of the metal trusses were already in place.

"Looks like a big warehouse to me."

"Yes, but it also looks like they're putting in a huge array of solar panels."

"Why's that a problem?"

"I'm just curious why they need that much electricity for an event center."

"Maybe they're trying to recoup some of their costs by selling electricity back to the utility company? I mean it's a huge space, plus you have the Bennett's old house, looks to be a few more going up…" She looked through the field glasses again. "And it looks like they've removed some trees in their backfield and mowed it down. It's covered in clover."

"Let me see." Carson scanned the property with the glasses. Finally, he sighed.

"Disappointed? What did you expect to find?"

"I don't know. I just think this has to have something to do with everything else going on."

"Are you ready to leave?"

"Yep. Come on." Crouching, they moved away from the top of the ridge until they felt confident no one could see them if there was anyone on watch.

He held her hand tightly as they slid and side-walked down the steep side and back to the trail. They had gone a short distance when they saw Mary jogging toward them.

She looked surprised to see them. "Well, hello. You're out early. She glanced toward the area they'd just come. What are you doing?"

"Birdwatching." Carson pulled the binoculars from his pocket. As if on cue, a bird flitted over to a branch on a tree.

"What's that one called?" Mary pointed.

Anne stumbled for words. Carson replied, "That's a common yellowthroat. Looks to be the male with that bright yellow on him."

"Yes, that's what I was going to say." Anne smiled at Mary. "Oh, I forgot my manners. Mary, this is Sheriff Carson. Ummm, I mean, Carson." Stumbling over her words, she said, "This is Mary Smith. She's staying at the Brandywine Inn now."

The woman reached over and shook Carson's hand with a firm grip. "Hello. Hope nothing's wrong out here?" she joked.

"No. Nothing." Anne took Carson's hand and slipped her other hand around his arm. "We're dating."

"Dating?" She surveyed them both.

"Yes, we've discovered we have a lot in common— like birdwatching."

"I see that black and white bird around a lot." She faced Anne.

Anne knew this one. "Ahh, the magpie. Some people often mistake it for our state bird."

"Which is what?"

"Lark Bunting." Carson responded.

Anne pointed to Carson. "He beat me to it. What I was going to say."

Mary said nothing but continued to survey the pair. Finally, she shook her legs and said, "I better get back to my run. Good seeing you. Have fun with your watching."

Anne and Carson watched as the woman jogged off in the distance.

"Did you feel like a kid who got caught with their hand in the cookie jar?" Anne wiped her brow.

"I felt something but more like I was being interrogated."

"I know what you mean. She has that vibe, right?" Anne took out a bottle and took a swig of water. "And her hanging out with Ruiz. Makes you wonder."

"It certainly does." He took her arm. "Pancakes or eggs?"

"Both!"

After they'd ordered pineapple pancakes, omelets, and hash browns, they sipped their drinks. He'd picked a coffee while Anne had selected a mimosa. They chatted about each other's life when they were younger and swapped stories as they enjoyed their meal.

"I want to make a pit stop before we head back to Carolan Springs. Okay with you?"

She nodded affirmation.

After Carson paid the check, they got in his rented vehicle and he drove toward the Botanical Gardens. As they passed it, he said, "Would you like to go there sometime? We could do the gardens and then dinner."

"Sounds nice." Anne watched as he turned onto Lincoln. "Where are we going?"

"Just a minute more."

They made a couple more turns and Anne realized where they were.

"The Sheriff's Department? You sure know how to show a girl a good time."

"I know someone in here and I need to check something out. Would you like to come in or wait out here?"

"If it's okay with you, I might stay out here." She reclined the seat back a bit and yawned.

"Okay, I shouldn't be too long. If it seems it will be longer than I think, I'll call you."

"Mm hm." She closed her eyes as the warm sun enveloped her.

"Lock the doors."

"Yes, sir." She saluted.

It seemed like a few minutes when he returned to the car. Anne wiped her eyes. "That didn't take long. Did you get what you need?"

"Yes. I think so. But now I'm even more curious about something. Is it okay if we take a ride past the Bennett place?"

"I don't have to be at the Inn today, so I'm all yours."

He smiled. "Good to know."

They drove out to the Bennett farm and as they approached Carson said, "I need to keep focused on the road and I don't want to stop the car, so tell me what you see. I'll slow down as much as I can without raising suspicion."

"Okay."

Carson had slowed the car to a speed that looked like a couple out enjoying the forest view. As they came around the corner, a huge gate appeared.

"Stewart wasn't joking when he said they'd put up a gate. Do they have T-Rex behind there?" Anne sat forward in her seat. As they drew closer, Anne's gaze traveled along the large wooden gate and to the pushbutton and call stand for entering the property. Then she saw it and gasped.

Carson turned to her. "What is it?"

"The gate. It has a large bull engraved in the wood."

Chapter Twenty-Three

They drove back by it but saw nothing else from the road. Carson dropped Anne at her house. "Is Spencer at the Inn today? Can we get him to come over here, so I can ask him some questions?"

"Shouldn't be a problem."

As Anne sat to take off her hiking boots, her cell phone rang.

"Hi, Hope. What's up?"

"We're going to have to cancel the bee-yard visit at Bill's."

"Oh, no. Why?"

"His hives have been destroyed. He's working now to try and gather the bees." Anne put the phone on speaker so Carson could hear. "I feel so sorry for him and Lori. They've been through so much."

"Carson and I will go over there right now." Anne looked up as Carson nodded assent. "What should we do in its place?"

"I called Susan, and we're going to go out to her house. She has beautiful herbal and floral gardens and we're going to talk about what to plant for bees and pollinators. The guests are looking forward to it. Then Bill said we can come out tomorrow as Nate has gone ahead and pulled the salvageable frames for extracting honey. The ones that are broken will be used to show how to get honey without an extractor."

"It sounds like you've got everything in hand. Carson and I will head over there right now and see if we can do anything to help." Anne canceled the call.

"Let's hold off on talking to Spencer until later. Maybe call him on the way and ask if he can come by this evening. Tell him I'll treat him to pizza."

"Not only do you know the key to a woman's heart but to a teenager's."

"I only want the key to one woman's heart." He reached over and clasped her hand.

Yikes. Things were moving fast. But were they? They'd known each other since right after she'd moved to Carolan Springs. They've probably gone through more together than some married couples.

Anne changed into a pair of Bob's shoes and they headed out to Bill's. Parking the car in the drive, they went around to the back. In the far corner, Carson and Anne watched as a few people in white jumpsuits with hooded veils were setting the hives back on cinder blocks. Parts of the hive were everywhere.

One of the figures looked up and waved. It was Bill. He headed over to them, taking his helmet off as he approached.

"Bill, I'm so sorry. Whatever happened?" Anne reached over and squeezed his arm.

He turned and looked back toward the hives. "We think it was a bear. I've been meaning to put up an electric fence but just never did. I feel we've encroached on their turf, but I never wanted to do anything that would harm them." He looked back at them. "I've lived here decades and never had an issue. Especially during the summer. I can understand it in spring or winter when they're either going in or out of hibernation, but it seems a weird time."

Carson spoke, "Bill, you sure it was a bear and not something else?"

Bill sighed, "You mean another vandalism?" He motioned to them to walk with him to the house. "I have to say it did cross my mind. But no, I'm going to say it was a bear." He shucked off his gloves and opened a back door that led into a lower storage room. They watched as Bill got out of his bee-suit and then followed him up the stairs.

"Lori isn't feeling too well today so she stayed in bed. But I'll let her know you're here." He went off down a hallway.

"Bears. That's all Bill needs." Anne went over and stood at the large picture window and watched as the beekeepers continued their work.

"I don't think it was a bear." Carson joined her.

She faced him. "Why do you say that? He believes it was a bear."

"No. What he said was 'I'm going to say it was a bear.' I need him to be straight with me. I've known him long enough to know he's hiding something. I may be Lori's cousin but I'm also still, at least in his eyes, the law. I think he's gotten involved in something that has turned nasty."

"Do you mean, you think Bill's involved in something illegal? No way. He'd never do that."

"Desperation can cause good people to do things they never imagined they would ever do."

Anne was going to respond when she heard a shuffling in the hallway. Bill had hold of Lori and she smiled wanly at them as she entered the room. Bill sat her down gingerly in the chair by the window.

"Lori, you make me feel bad. We wouldn't expect you to get out of bed for us."

The frail woman shook her head. "No. It's okay. I was ready to get out of that bed. It's better for me if I move around, even if it's for a little bit."

Carson came over and planted a kiss on her head. "Lori." He bent down and held her hand. The silence stretched between them, yet it seemed as if they'd both spoken volumes.

Bill grimaced as he touched the back of his head.

"How's the head healing coming?" Anne took a seat on the sofa. Carson sat down next to her.

"Pretty good. I still have some headaches and twinges, but the doctor says that's to be expected and can take months, if not years, before they disappear."

"Is there anything we can do to help? Please." Anne clasped her hands together in her lap.

"We're fine," Lori spoke softly. "I know it doesn't look like it, but I went to the doctor this week and they say I'm doing better."

"That's wonderful news," Anne exclaimed.

Carson replied, "What's next for you?"

"The doctor said to keep doing what I'm doing." Her eyes went to Bill.

"Don't you worry. I'm going to make sure you have what you need. I'll do whatever it takes."

At Bill's statement, Anne glanced over at Carson. She knew his statement had registered, but Carson didn't look back at her.

Carson stood up. "We should be going. We just stopped by to see if we can help." He went over and shook Bill's hand before grabbing him into one of those slap-on-the-back hugs favored by men.

Anne heard Carson say, "Bill, I got your back. Don't do anything I wouldn't do."

Bill swallowed. "My only goal is taking care of Lori."

"And I know you will. But know that others can help."

Bill walked over and stood by Lori's chair. She reached up and took his hand. "You all are so thoughtful to come out and ask if we need help. I hope you'll take my advice. Cherish each other."

The surprise must have shown on Anne's face.

Lori smiled, "It's been evident since I first saw you together. You belong together. You're a fit. If you want to do something for me—please love each other." She broke off as a coughing fit took hold. She clutched at her chest. "Enough talking for now, I think."

Anne came over and kissed Lori goodbye and gave Bill a hug. They drove away from the home in silence.

It's so easy to take life for granted. Bill and Lori have seen how truly precious it is.

Anne stole a glance at Carson, his face deep in concentration. She did love him. Probably had for a while.

He turned to her and she knew he had been thinking the same thing.

Chapter Twenty-Four

Carson dropped Anne at her house and then went home to shower and grab a pizza for dinner. Anne had called Spencer, who asked if he could bring a friend or two. A few pizzas had grown to a large stack, and Anne chuckled as she opened the back door to let Carson in with his arms loaded down with pizzas.

"You look like you're going to feed an army."

"Teenagers are an army. An army of hormones, usually."

"Boy, don't I remember."

A knock came to the back door and Spencer entered with two kids Anne didn't know and one she did.

"Missy! So nice to see you. How's your mother?" Anne recalled that Missy's mom, Sorcha, had dated Carson for a while. She guessed that Sorcha had decided he wasn't the one for her.

"She's well. Thanks for asking, Ms. Freemont." She stood awkwardly at the door until Spencer pulled out a chair for her to sit down.

Spencer spoke, "This is Ron, and this is Carrie."

Another knock sounded on the door. A young man a bit older than the others stood there. "Hi, I'm Peter. I heard there was pizza here for foster kids."

Spencer crossed his arms. "Not for just anyone."

Carson put his hand on Spencer's shoulder. "Yes, it's for anyone who wants some. Come in."

The attractive blond teen came in and took a seat next to Missy. "Hello."

She giggled back at him. "Hi."

Spencer huffed and moved over to another chair. Evidently, Spencer had a crush on Missy and Peter was causing a problem.

Anne cocked her head for Carson to follow her out of the room.

"Do you have enough pizza, or do I need to order more?"

"I think we'll be fine, but poor Spence. He's definitely got a touch of puppy love. How much older is Missy—three, four years?"

"I think so. But you know what they say, it may be puppy love but it sure is real to that puppy."

He chuckled. "True." He reached up and pushed a stray lock behind her ear.

Anne shooed his hand away. "We need to get back in there. Are you sure this is going to work? I don't know if we can really ask Spencer anything with this many teens?"

"You never know. We'll play it by ear." He stiffened up. "Ready for combat?"

"Yes."

In the kitchen, the teens had all taken seats and were eyeing the pizza boxes.

"My bad. I should have said to dig in." Carson opened them up on the counter while Anne pulled sodas from the refrigerator. "I've got pepperoni, cheese, veggie and I forgot what this one is but it's a bunch of meat with other toppings."

Everyone dug in and the teens talked about being able to sleep in and what jobs they'd found for the summer months. Carson and Anne took their places and listened to the teen's banter back and forth.

As soon as everyone had eaten, Anne spoke.

"I…we've invited you here because we need your help."

Spencer leaned forward in his chair. "Is this another case you need us to help with?"

Carson replied, "No—"

Anne patted his hand and smiled up at him, sending the clear message to let her handle it.

"What Sheriff Carson means is that we do need your help but just not in any way other than giving us information."

Peter slumped back in his chair, scowling and crossing his arms. "We ain't no narcs."

"Funny you should use that term, Peter. Can you tell me why you used it?" Anne waited.

Peter licked his lips and glanced nervously between Anne and Carson.

"You better say what you know. I saw you smoking pot with Ray." Carrie chimed in.

Peter sprung up from his chair. "I don't have to—"

"Sit. Down." Carson's authoritative voice commanded obedience.

Eyes like big saucers watched as Peter returned to his seat.

"I'm not here to catch you out, though I think you're stupid for doing any drugs." Carson laid his hands on the table. "We simply want you to answer some questions."

Peter nodded, and Carson looked at the others, who quickly followed suit.

"Now, and no lies. I can spot them in an instant."

"He can too. He told me…" Spencer puffed up.

"Thanks." Carson responded.

Anne spoke to the group. "We know that Ray Lawrence was dealing drugs."

Carrie piped up. "He tried to get me to do it, but that stuff is gross. But I saw Pete and Ron out with Ray."

Ron stiffened. "I only did it once. Just to try it. Ray… and him"—he nodded toward Peter—"said they could get me set up selling to kids in the school. Easy money."

"Is that so?" Carson turned back to Peter.

"Okay. Fine. Juvie's better than old lady Lawrence's place." He slumped down further. "Ray came and said that he could get me hooked up with a lady—"

"Wait. A lady?" Anne interrupted and was quickly reminded by Carson's squeeze to not interrupt again.

She turned to Carson. "Sorry, my bad."

"As you were saying, Ray said he would introduce you to a lady." Carson motioned him to continue.

Anne had to get him to answer. "How long ago was it that he said he would have you meet this woman?"

As Peter thought about it Missy said, "Well, I'm glad Doug is leaving soon."

Ron replied, "He already left. He told me that he scored a great deal of making some fast money."

Anne tried not to roll her eyes. What happened to these guys' work ethic?

"He asked me out, but he gave me the creeps." Missy added.

"How was—Doug, was it? Going to make this fast cash? Selling drugs?"

"Naw. He was supposed to get back at some old dude. Mess up his car as much as possible."

Anne's jaw dropped. Doug had been the one to destroy Carson's car. Then he'd left town.

"Did he say who hired him?"

"No. He said the messages were relayed through other kids and he never met the guy. He did show me the last note from the guy. Scary."

Anne sat forward. "What did it say?"

"Do it tonight. Don't get caught. If you get caught or you say anything, we'll kill you. We can get to you."

"Yikes."

"Do you still have the note?" Carson asked Ron.

"I never had it. I guess he either took it with him or threw it away."

Carson turned back to Peter. "Okay, back to the woman."

"Yeah. Like I said, I was told she'd hook me up with …hmmm, stuff, that I could sell to the high school kids and anyone else. I don't have much longer, and I've got to make a living. Easy money."

Anne started. "Not much longer?"

"He means under foster care. Correct?" Carson addressed the surly young man.

"Right. No money. I need something soon."

Anne laughed. "You ever heard of getting a job?"

Peter shook his head. "No way. I'm planning on working smarter not harder."

Anne stopped the groan from leaving her mouth.

"Okay. Ray was going to introduce you to a woman that was going to get you fixed up to sell drugs. Did you ever meet this woman?"

"No. Ray was killed, and then the next thing I know, all these cops are over at Ms. Lawrence's."

"I remember that," Ron spoke up. "They asked Ms. Lawrence if Ray stayed there and they wanted to search his room. My room is down in the basement with Pete, and Ray used to stay in the other room if there wasn't another foster kid. You know, boys downstairs, girls upstairs."

Peter said, "I heard them talking. I think one guy was the police chief. I couldn't hear much of what they said but they kept saying it was bull."

"Bull?" Anne glanced over at Carson and he gestured not to reveal anything.

"Anything else?"

"Naw. I heard them moving around in the room, pulling out stuff. But they didn't say much else. What was funny though was that police officer had the same name as that woman Ray talked about."

Anne leaned closer. "What was the name Ray mentioned?"

Peter slumped further down in his chair. "I think it was something like Smith."

Chapter Twenty-Five

The kids had said they had to get back, so they all walked to the front door. Anne grabbed Spencer's arm.

"Spence, you're not, I mean, you wouldn't do drugs."

"Don't worry, Miss Anne. I'm smarter than that."

"I apologize. I know you are. Just a bit worried, I guess."

Spencer hugged her. "It's nice having somebody worry about me." He waved as he sprinted to catch up with the others. "Got to go. Later."

Carson came back into the kitchen. "I don't know about you, but I could go for a drink."

"Like?"

"Got any Scotch?"

Anne shook her head. "Sorry. I've got wine or beer."

He sighed. "Merlot at least?"

"Yes." She pulled a bottle from a cabinet and he uncorked it with ease. She set out two glasses and he poured them.

"Want to sit out on the porch?"

"Sounds good." He opened the door for her as they walked out on the porch. They each took a spot on the glider and for a while, neither spoke.

Finally, Anne turned to Carson. "There's so much to think about. We've got the situation with Ray. Then the woman. The bull has to mean that the police know about El Toro. Plus, we need to find out what officer has the same name as the woman. How many female police officers are in Carolan Springs?"

"I don't know. I can easily find out. But I can go over tomorrow and get it."

Anne took a sip of the wine, enjoying its smoky, aged flavor. "I want to say something, and I want you to hear me out."

"Okay. Is this from Anne or ND?"

She stuck out her tongue at him. "One and the same. Plus, we're back to you not giving me your name."

"I told you. It's Carson."

Anne growled. "I'm not going to be mad at you right now. Maybe later. We have to get this figured out."

"Okay." He grinned over his wine glass. "But you really shouldn't be mad."

"I choose when and if I'll be mad, thank you very much."

"Your prerogative." He raised his glass.

"Be serious. Here's the thing. We have information that a woman is involved and also someone who's name is El Toro. Who does that remind you of?"

Carson quickly sobered. "Are you referring to Ruiz? Just because he has a Hispanic name?"

"Well, we can't rule him out."

"Fair enough. And the woman?"

"What about Mary Smith? I mean, come on. That's got to be a fake name. And I've seen her with Ruiz."

"Okay, so let's think about that. She could be using another name because she wants to. No law against it."

"But why would you do that unless you're a celebrity? As far as I know, she doesn't look like anyone I've seen on TV, in movies or online."

"Big tabloid watcher, are we?"

"No. But I do love movies. And plays."

"We've gotten off track."

"Okay, so can we agree that they could have something to do with it? I mean, I've seen that Mary carries a gun and she always seems to be around. In fact, don't turn your head, but she's watching us right now from the Inn."

"She may be watching us, or she may have just noticed us." He turned and faced toward the Inn. "Hello. Care to join us?"

Anne watched as Mary, now dressed in a simple dress and sandals made her way across the two connecting drives. She came up the porch steps. "Sorry, I didn't mean to intrude. I was wanting to talk with you about something and didn't know how to go about it. I guess I'd gotten lost in my thoughts. I didn't mean to be staring. Honestly."

"Would you like a glass of wine?"

"If it's not too much bother."

Anne replied no and went to the kitchen for another goblet and the bottle of wine. After she'd poured some for Mary, she topped up Carson's glass and then her own.

Mary took a sip. "I, well, I have no right to ask. But I saw all those kids leaving your house. I overheard them talking about drugs and El Toro and it, to be honest, freaked me out a bit. I may have to rethink running by myself." She waited for their reply.

"It's perfectly safe here," Carson replied.

"You're the sheriff in town? Correct?" Mary raised the glass to her lips but stopped before taking a sip.

"I am."

"Do you—"

"Miss Smith. Why are you here?" Carson responded, setting his glass down on the corner table.

"I'm here for a vacation."

"Why did you choose Carolan Springs?"

She smiled at them. "I've always wanted to visit Colorado and I went online and found this place. I figured it would be a nice, relaxing time here."

"How long do you intend to stay?"

Mary hesitated. "I'm not sure, yet. Why do you ask?"

"It must be nice to extend your time away from your job. What is it you do?"

There was no hesitation this time as she responded, "I'm a trainer. When my clients are away, it gives me a chance to take time off."

"I don't know that many trainers. But not many carry guns." He waited for her response.

She set her glass down, untouched. "I carry for protection. I train in that area."

Anne wanted so badly to say, "Honestly, come clean. Why are you here?" But she held her tongue.

The silence stretched.

"This has been really nice chatting with you." Mary stood. She thanked Anne and left the porch.

Carson also stood. "I need to be going as well." He turned to face her. "Lots to think about. I'm going to be out of town tomorrow morning. Have to go up to Denver for a talk with the state's sheriff's office. I should be back by the afternoon." He stepped over to her. "What will you be doing while I'm away for the day?"

"I have Inn duties tomorrow, so sticking close to home. When you're done, stop by and let me know what happened."

"I will."

"And just so we can put this to bed, my name is Carson. Carson Vlk. No one could ever understand my name. I made it simple by using my first name instead. Happy now?"

She laughed. "Yes."

He tilted her chin and kissed her goodnight. "Sweet dreams."

"You too." Anne watched as Carson got into his vehicle and drove away.

She sighed with contentment. Even after all that she'd gone through with her ex, there'd constantly been something that didn't quite click. She'd always felt on edge, never comfortable or safe like she did with Carson. Though she was still unsure about where their relationship was heading, she knew one thing for sure. She had to clear Carson's name. The only person she felt could help was Officer Dale. She was going to call him first thing tomorrow morning.

Chapter Twenty-Six

When Anne arrived at the Inn the next morning, Kandi was already prepping everything for breakfast.

"Morning!" Kandi called out.

"Ugh. Too early. How can you be so chipper when it's dark-o-thirty?" Anne shuffled over to the coffee pot and made herself an espresso.

"It's six o'clock. I've been up since five. I let my girls out and checked on Boo Bear."

Kandi had chickens and had taken to the large Newfoundland that they'd helped rescue. He would often hang out at her house in the evenings and Kandi liked that his presence seemed to keep predators away from her girls.

Anne frothed some cream and poured it over the espresso. She added a sprinkling of raw sugar on top.

Kandi giggled. "You must be tired if you're adding sugar to your coffee."

Anne sat down. "I think I'm mentally tired more than anything. Trying to figure out what's going on had me tossing and turning all night."

"You sure it wasn't, *like,* thinking about a certain someone that kept you awake?" She finished putting the homemade biscuits onto a pan, which was now ready to slide into the oven.

"I'm pretty sure it wasn't that." Although, truth be told, thoughts of Carson weighed on her mind. They certainly weren't school kids, but where were they going with the relationship? She knew one thing, she didn't want to be hurt again. Anne took a swig of the warm liquid, enjoying the rich taste.

"I've got paperwork this morning. Anything you need me to do to help with breakfast first?"

Kandi slid the biscuits into the oven. "Could you squeeze some oranges?"

"Sure." Anne gathered up the box of oranges and used the juicer. The rhythm of the handheld pump was soothing. The pair worked in companionable silence, Anne with the juicer and Kandi creating individual bowls of ingredients for omelets the guests had ordered last night.

The back door opened. It was Hope. "Morning, Hope. I didn't think you were coming over today."

"Spencer is going to show me something on the computer later, to help with ordering. Since there's so much racket with the remodel of the shop, I said I'd meet him over here."

"At this hour? I thought teenagers were like vampires. They hated the morning sun." Anne chuckled.

"He's trying to save up to get a laptop. He said he'd be here early as that lets him get his chores done here and then work almost a full-day at Patty's Pet Shop."

"I wish his work ethic would rub off on some of those other kids." Anne pulled the shell of the orange off the juicer.

Hope sat down. "What do you mean?"

Anne recounted what the teens had said the evening before. Kandi and Hope both listened intently.

"Whoa. That sounds, *like,* weird. Do you really think Mary Smith is not who she says she is?"

"That's just the thing. She has never said who she is. And seriously, Mary Smith? I could have come up with a better name than that."

Hope helped Anne as she filtered the juice from the orange pips. "It seems strange. But I would think she'd want to remain out of sight if she's really part of this drug operation."

"Maybe she's trying to hide in plain sight." Anne transferred the juice to a large container with a spout. Cutting some oranges thinly, she added them to the container. "I need to wash my hands. They're still sticky. Then I can take this into the dining room."

"I'll take it. I thought I heard some of the guests. I think I'm more awake for morning banter than you are." Hope picked up the container.

Anne folded her hands in a prayer posture. "Thank you, my child. I am not for morning banter this morning. Be blessed."

"You goof." Hope walked out of the kitchen.

Chapter Twenty-Seven

After Kandi had assured Anne that she had everything under control, Anne went into the office and shut the door behind her. She opened the desk drawer and rummaged through a stack of cards until she found the one Officer Dale had provided.

The call went to voicemail, so she called the station. A woman's voice answered. When she informed Anne that Officer Dale wasn't in, she asked if someone else could help. Anne said, "Could I speak with Police Chief Everett?"

The woman officer responded, "Can I say what this is about?"

Anne hesitated, then said, "Tell him it's about El Toro."

The line clicked off and Anne waited. In a moment, a strong male voice came on the line. "Ms. Freemont. How can I help you?"

Anne told him about her ideas, about the talk last night with the teens, about seeing the bull on the front gate at the Bennett's place, and about the woman. She didn't say she suspected Mary Smith or Deputy Ruiz. "I think someone framed Carson to get him out of the way."

"I hate to admit it Ms. Freemont, but I have to agree. What does Sheriff Carson say about you speaking with me?"

"Oh, he doesn't know I'm talking to you. I was trying to get ahold of Officer Dale but he's not answering his phone right now."

"Have you spoken to anyone else about this?"

"Just my friends."

She waited while silence sounded in her ear. Finally, Chief Everett spoke. "Ms. Freemont, we could be dealing with very dangerous people who will stop at nothing to hide what they're doing. You can't take chances. I thank you for telling me all of this, but you need to stay out of it. Safer for you and safer for your friends."

"But—"

"You've been extremely helpful. I'll connect with Officer Dale."

"Are you going to go out to the Bennett place and look around?" She changed the phone to her other ear.

"Ms. Freemont, the Bennett place is out of our jurisdiction. It's not in the city, it's in the county, so is under the sheriff's department. But I have a good connection with someone over there, so I'll have them check it out."

"You mean Deputy Ruiz?"

"What makes you say that?"

"No reason."

"Ms. Freemont, Thank you for calling me. I'd also take what those teens say with a grain of salt. They often embellish things to get more attention or to act bigger in front of their peers."

"I don't think—"

"I work with those kids all the time. I know. Trust me."

For some reason, his attitude toward the foster kids made Anne bristle. You couldn't lump all these kids into one category. If they acted out, certainly the reasons behind them being placed in foster care might have something to do with it.

He continued, "I have to end the call, but please call me with anything else that you may think of that will assist us." The line went dead.

Anne sat and stared at her phone. "I think I've been dismissed." Her anger grew. She got up and paced up and down the room. "I should have waited and talked with Officer Dale. He wouldn't have treated me so rudely."

Anne hadn't heard Hope come down the hall or open the door. "Talking to our self again?" Hope came over and sat down at the desk.

"Done here?"

"Go ahead. I can do what I need in a little while." Hope slumped down in a chair. "What is it?" Hope turned toward Anne.

"I hate being treated like I'm an idiot. Every time I get off the phone with these people, I feel like someone just patted me on the head and said, 'thanks dear, now go play with your toys.' It's so frustrating."

"Don't let it get to you. It will all work out."

"I wish I could be as calm as you, Hope." Anne ran her fingers through her hair. "Ugh. I'm sorry. Here I am going on about this stupidity when you've got the remodel because of the fire and caring for your mom."

"It's okay. But thank you. I know Carson didn't do it, but I don't have answers to why they found items at his house that connected to the fire. It's making me doubt myself and I don't like it."

"I know. You don't think he's been lying to us all the time, do you?"

Hope sighed. "I know I always trust my gut. If I don't trust mine, I trust Mama's. She's always liked Sheriff Carson."

"But she said it was the sheriff that came and got her away from the house."

Hope looked up and groaned. "How could I have missed it? I can't believe I didn't think about it sooner."

"Are you going to let me in on what you're talking about?"

"Sheriff. She called him sheriff, but it didn't mean it was the sheriff. Anyone could be in a uniform and say he's the sheriff if she asked."

"But wouldn't she know it wasn't Carson? Hope, I think we need to talk to your mom."

"Okay, but it will have to be after Spencer's gone."

"I have some things to do too, but I can do them later. Let me know when you're ready."

"Will do. Shouldn't be too long."

Anne's phone rang. She mouthed 'see you later' to Hope and walked out of the room. It was Officer Dale.

"Hello?"

"This Ms. Freemont?"

"Yes."

"Are you alone?" What a strange question.

"Yes." She had some time to kill, so she headed out to the gazebo in the back as she talked.

"I need to see you. I think some of the information that you provided may be critical."

"I can come into the station this afternoon."

"No. Not the station. Do you know the old Silver Camp Road?"

Anne recalled the old road that was rarely used except by four-wheelers and hikers. "I know it, but why—"

"I'm concerned for your safety. I don't want anyone to see us talking to one another. Don't tell anyone you're coming to meet me."

"Okay. What time?"

"This afternoon. How about three?"

"I can do that. I'll meet you there at three. Silver Camp Road. By the old homestead." She hung up the phone.

"Who are you meeting at Silver Camp Road at three?" Carson's voice cut through the silence.

Anne screamed. "You scared me to death. Don't do that!"

"Okay. But answer my question. Who was that and why are you meeting them in such a secluded place?"

"It was Officer Dale. He wants me to meet him out there."

"Why?"

"I guess Chief Everett told him what I said."

"What you said?"

"Yes. I tried calling Dale but spoke to Chief Everett instead."

Carson sighed. "ND, you're killing me. How can I protect you if you keep putting yourself in harm's way?"

"They're the police. Plus, I didn't tell them everything. I left out the information about Mary and Ruiz."

"Well, at least there's that. Call Officer Dale back and tell him you're not coming."

"I am."

"You're not."

"Yes. I. Am." She crossed her arms. "He said that we needed to meet out there because he was concerned for my safety. He didn't want me going to the station or being seen talking to the police."

Carson rubbed his chin. "Possible. But I still don't like it. I'm coming with you."

"I don't think that's necessary, but I'll be glad for the company."

Carson said he'd be back at two thirty and they could drive out together. The rest of the morning passed slowly. At two o'clock, Carson returned and had changed into a brown shirt and slacks. He waited for Anne to finish her work.

"Let's take your car. He'll be expecting it."

Anne swept up her keys and purse. "Okay. I'm ready."

Carson was quiet as they made their way out of town. Little by little, the distance between houses grew longer until they were surrounded by forested land on both sides.

"There it is." Carson pointed to an old worn sign, the paint barely readable. Anne turned off onto the dirt road. It was slow going as they climbed higher and higher up the mountain, each bend in the curve steeper than the last.

"I hate driving up in the mountains. You should have driven."

"Just remember to keep it in low gear and don't ride your brakes."

"I know that. I'm more concerned about those drop-offs."

They rounded the next bend and saw a police cruiser. "That must be Dale's."

Carson motioned for Anne to pull over closer to the mountain.

"Stay here."

As she grabbed the door jam, Anne heard tires grabbing on gravel. Someone was coming up behind them. Had they been followed?

Carson had heard too and moved in front of the vehicle.

Another police cruiser appeared. An officer not familiar to Anne pulled up next to them.

"Where's the Chief?"

"What?" Anne got out on her side and moved next to Carson. The officer got out of his vehicle, but Anne noticed he kept his hand on his gun. What was going on?

A male voice punctuated the air. "I'm here."

They all swiveled to see Chief Everett climb up over the edge of the road. They walked toward him as he called to the officer, "Newton, call in dispatch. Officer down." The officer went back to his cruiser.

He turned to Anne and Carson. "It's Dale. He's dead."

Chapter Twenty-Eight

"Dead?" Anne couldn't believe it. "But when? How?"

Chief Everett took off his hat, wiped his head and replaced it on his head. "Dale told me was coming out to meet you. He'd already left, and I told him to get back to the station. But he said he was almost here and once he saw you, he'd have you come back with him. I didn't like it, so I came out here. I couldn't see his vehicle, so I walked along the side. That's when I looked down and saw his cruiser."

Anne and Carson walked over to the edge of the road. The cruiser had plowed through scrub oak, and smaller ponderosa pines bore the marks of broken branches and trunks.

"The only thing I can figure out is that he took the corner too fast and over-corrected."

Anne started to speak but Carson grabbed her hand and squeezed it.

"I hoped that he was only hurt, but when I got there, he was dead." Chief Everett looked at Anne. "Did he tell you what he wanted to talk to you about?"

Anne shook her head. "No. I figured it was about what I'd already told you."

"Well, we'll never know now. I'm sad to have him leave my team."

"You think it was an accident?" Anne put her hand up and shielded her eyes from the sun.

He didn't reply at first. "We must wait for the techs to tell us. Why?"

"I'm just wondering if El Toro had him killed."

"Why do you say that?"

"Maybe he knew who El Toro is."

"Good point." He looked toward the wreckage below. "You know, Dale had been acting strange lately. I'd attributed it to just the job. It gets to you sometimes. Right, Carson?"

Carson nodded in affirmation. "Yes. It can."

"I asked him about it, but the only thing I found out was that he'd gotten into debt. I think he'd been doing some gambling or something over in Cripple Creek. Lost a ton of money." He stopped. "No. I can't believe he'd..."

He didn't finish the sentence, but he didn't have to. Had Dale gotten mixed up with El Toro to make money? Had he been turning information over but then El Toro had decided he was a liability? Had Dale meant to tell them who El Toro was and been killed before he got the chance?

"Chief Everett, is it okay if I take Anne home?" Carson inquired.

"Yes. Sure. We know where to find you. Please don't speak about this to anyone before we notify his family and the media releases the information. I'd take it as a personal favor."

"Certainly." Carson guided Anne back to the car, opening the door to the passenger seat. Inside, he made a three-point turn as he glimpsed city vehicles coming up the road on the other switchback. Anne glanced over her shoulder and watched as Chief Everett disappeared back down the hill.

They passed the caravan of police vehicles going up the hill and drove in silence to town. Once they hit the main street, Anne asked if Carson would stop by Hope's. She wanted to see the new features being put in that Hope had told her about. He pulled into a parking spot and got out. After checking out the new shelving to house all the herbs for sale and use, Carson recommended an early supper.

"I'm good with that," Anne said, linking her arm in his. They had made it to the vehicle when Kandi pulled up in her bright red truck. They waited as she lowered the window. "I'm here to pick up Stewart and we're heading over to Franco's for dinner. Want to join us?"

Anne looked at Carson. "What do you say?"

"Sounds good."

Stewart appeared from the alleyway. Hope must have let him use her shower up in her loft apartment, because he didn't look like he'd been doing carpentry all day. "Coming with?"

"Yes." Anne moved toward her car, but Kandi stopped her. "Why don't you come with us and I'll drop you back at your car later."

"That works." Carson opened the back passenger door and Anne slid across the seat. Once Carson was in the truck, Anne told Kandi and Stewart about Officer Dale.

"That's horrible." Stewart twisted to face Carson and Anne. "Do you think it was an accident or something else?"

"I don't know. We aren't to tell anyone, so this can't leave this cab."

"Mouth sealed." Stewart drew a zip across his mouth. "It seems, I don't know, off."

"That's what I was thinking too," Carson replied.

Anne turned to face him. "What do you mean?"

"He was supposed to meet us. But then he's killed—accidentally or otherwise. Why there and why now?"

"I guess you're right, but maybe he figured out something from what we'd told him."

"Could be." Carson rested his arm on the back seat. "We'll find out more once the autopsy's performed."

"We're here!" Kandi chirped.

They pulled into a spot close to the door, the parking lot already filling up with patrons.

"They have the yummiest Italian food. It's, *like*, so good."

"It is good." Carson stepped out of the truck and put out his hand for Anne to exit.

Kandi and Stewart were chatting ahead of them with Carson and Anne following.

"Stop!" Anne commanded as she grabbed Carson's arm. Kandi and Stewart turned around too.

"Did you forget something?" Stewart asked.

"No. I remembered something I wanted to tell Carson. You two go on ahead and get us a table. We'll be in there in a minute."

"Okay." Kandi bounced toward the door, reminding Anne of a human Tigger.

Carson looked down at Anne. "What it is?"

"Walk with me back to the truck and act like we're looking to see if I left something in there."

"Okay, but what's with all the subterfuge, ND?"

Anne took his arm. "You'll see. When we're coming back, just glance around the parking lot, especially to the back area to the left, but don't stop."

"Now you've got me curious." Carson stopped next to Anne as she made the pretense of looking in Kandi's windows.

"Nope. I must have left it in my car." Anne turned, and they walked back toward the restaurant.

Anne knew Carson had seen what she intended when his breath caught for a second.

"Got it?" She asked him.

"Yes." He placed his hand on her back to lead her inside. Once inside, they looked at one another but said nothing. After he'd seated Anne, he excused himself. When he returned, he leaned over and whispered to Anne. "Look."

She glanced down to where he held his phone. The picture on it was unmistakable. Deputy Ruiz's vehicle had a smashed front fender and white paint streaks.

"White paint," Anne said under her breath.

Carson nodded. He didn't need to respond. They both knew the town 's police cars were white.

News traveled quickly in Carolan Springs, but when the town's paper came out, the headline shocked the small town.

Sheriff's Deputy Takes Own Life.

Police Chief Bradley Everett released a formal statement. "We are extremely saddened at the loss of one of our officers. And in this tragic manner. Our condolences to his family and friends at this tragic time."

Sam had stopped by Anne's where Carson, Hope, Stewart, and Kandi had already gathered.

"Can you share anything with us, Sam?" Carson requested.

"As far as it looks, he tried to kill himself by going off the road to make it look like an accident. But it only injured him. He used his service revolver." Sam shook his head. "He really seemed like a nice guy. But now—"

Hope asked, "What do you mean 'but now'?"

"Unofficially, they've found all kinds of incriminating evidence at his house connecting him to the arsons in the area. They think he craved the attention and appreciation. But they also found things linking him to the drug cartel. In fact, he had a tattoo of a bull on his chest."

"He did?" Anne scooted forward.

"Yes. Lots of information about El Toro at his place."

"Do you think he was El Toro?" Stewart questioned.

Sam shook his head. "I don't know. I wouldn't think so. But who better to keep things under wraps than someone on the force?"

Anne and Carson exchanged glances but said nothing.

Had Ruiz gotten Dale to work for him? Had Dale decided to spill the beans about Ruiz?

The doorbell rang. Anne went to answer it and found Police Chief Everett standing at the door.

"Chief. Please," she said, waving her hand, "come in."

"I can only stay a moment. I wanted to stop by since you and Sheriff Carson were there when we found Officer Dale."

"He's in the kitchen. Follow me."

In the kitchen, Anne introduced everyone to Chief Everett. "I'm sorry to interrupt you. I wanted to stop by and thank Anne for her information. I should have followed up on it sooner." He turned to Carson. "All charges against you have been dropped. I would think you'd be reinstated soon."

"Would you like to sit down?" Stewart got up from his chair.

"No thanks. I can only stay a moment. I have to say, I think Dale was a good guy. I sent him out to look at the Bennett's place like you suggested, Ms. Freemont. It wasn't long after that... well, you know."

"It's so sad. Why would he do that?"

"I don't know. Too many questions and not enough answers. I can't believe someone involved him in something like that. And his car. Makes no sense. It looks more like an accident. Maybe he thought no one would find him. He was too injured to move so maybe he chose to end it."

"Couldn't he have called for help?"

"Coverage is sporadic at best up in the mountains. Plus, his radio could have been broken. They haven't finished going over the vehicle yet."

Carson stood. "Thanks for coming by, Chief. I'm glad we've settled this. Ray and Dale must have thought they could turn a quick buck. I'm glad it's over now." He shook the chief's hand.

"Agreed." Everett turned to the group. "Well, I've got to get on."

Anne walked him to the door. Returning to the kitchen she said, "Is it really over?"

"Oh yes, it's over," Carson stated emphatically.

Chapter Twenty-Nine

After everyone had left, Carson told Anne he'd see her tomorrow. Mouser let her know in his plaintive meows that she had been neglecting him.

Anne took time to do housekeeping chores she'd been overlooking, her mind occupied as she worked.

How could it be over? Certainly, Dale wasn't El Toro. What about Ruiz? His car bore the proof that he'd hit something and damaged the fender. Then there was the woman the teens all spoke about. Was that Mary Smith? She and Ruiz had definitely been seen together. And she was always evasive about why she had come to Carolan Springs and what she did for a living. Most people were more forthcoming.

Then there was Bill. Why would Dale have harmed him? For a few measly pot plants? Made little sense. Anne knew Carson felt Bill wasn't being truthful about the reason for the attack, but Bill was remaining quiet. Was Dale the reason?

Then there was the Bennett place. Had Dale killed Ray?

Anne switched off the vacuum. "Ugh. I'm not getting anywhere with this."

A thought came to mind. She'd head over to see Lori and find out if they'd heard about Dale. Maybe Bill would be more forthcoming with Dale out of the picture.

Anne went out into the backyard to her floral cutting garden. It was one of the first things she'd added to the backyard, as she wanted to have fresh-cut flowers in the house. She decided on some big, puffy teddy-bear sunflowers. Inside, she stuck them in a large mason jar and wrapped the jar with raffia ribbon. She pulled out a label and wrote, "To Sunny Days Ahead."

Anne got in her car and drove out to Bill and Lori's. But when she arrived, the couple was out. She walked around to the back, but they weren't there. After leaving the flowers on the doorstep with a note, Anne got back into her vehicle.

Tapping her fingers on the wheel, she thought about her next steps. She'd backed out of the driveway and decided she'd see if Sam had learned anything else. Carson may think it was over, but it was far from over in Anne's mind.

She enjoyed the drive out to Sam's. But when she made her way up his drive, she found that she wasn't the only one who had paid Sam a visit. Ruiz's truck was parked under a tree.

Anne pulled up to a stop and exited the vehicle when she saw Ruiz. He was coming from the back deck. He started when he saw Anne. He advanced toward her. "Hey, you out to go fishing?"

"I'm looking for Sam."

A woman's voice answered. "He's not here. He went into town to grab a few things."

Anne watched as Mary Smith descended the few steps and walked over to her.

"Oh. Well. Okay." Anne stumbled for something to say.

"Ruiz, that's it, correct?" Mary turned to him.

"Yes, you're right."

She continued, "He'd come out to go fishing but no luck. Right?"

Anne wasn't that dumb. Most people would fish early morning on the lake or later in the day. Not in the afternoon's heat when the fish went deeper, but she said nothing.

"Yep. Looks like hamburgers for dinner." He turned to the woman. "If you'll let Sam know I stopped by and said hi."

"Be glad to." She beamed at him.

Wow. Could the acting get any worse? Was Mary playing the field with Sam and Ruiz? Anne couldn't care less. She hoped that was what was going on and not that Ruiz and Mary were involved in a drug cartel.

"Yes. Let Sam know I stopped by." Anne quickly got back in her vehicle and headed home.

Dead ends. Everywhere she turned. More dead ends.

She slammed on her brakes. Looking up in the mirror she was glad she was the only one on the road.

Dead End. That's what Dale's death had provided. Someone had been leading them to think they were at the end.

She put her foot on the gas.

Once Anne got back into town, a rush of firetrucks went by, sirens blaring. Behind them a deputy's car followed by an ambulance.

She wondered what was happening. It was rare to see such a sight of all the town's public safety vehicles in such a hurry.

The hair on her arms stood up. She flipped her car around and followed behind the ambulance. Alarms continued as they turned off the main street toward the feeder for Old Ranch Road.

Carson lived off Old Ranch Road.

She kept pace behind the vehicles and her fear grew as the smell of smoke filtered in through her vehicle's air ducts. Off to the right, flames were licking at the base of trees. She pulled her SUV off to the side and opened her door. The firetrucks were spraying down the forest as the wildfire management crew set to digging in boundary lines.

She slammed the door shut and rushed toward the driveway that led to what had once been a home. Fire engulfed the entire structure.

"No!" She stifled a scream. Where was Carson? She hunted frantically for him among the many male faces.

A deputy came toward her. "Ma'am, you can't be here. You will have to leave."

She shrugged away from his touch. "No. I'm not leaving until I see Carson. Where is he?" She stifled another cry as she repeated, "Where is he?"

"The firefighters are searching where they can, but…"

He didn't need to finish the statement. There was no way anyone inside the structure that was now engulfed in flames would have survived.

Anne broke down in sobs. She felt sick. Anne bent over, clutching her knees, trying to steady herself.

They called the deputy over by a firefighter and he motioned for one of the EMTs to see to her.

It was Sam who came over. "Anne, what are you doing here?"

"I… I…"

"Let's have you sit down. Okay?"

She nodded. He wrapped an arm around her and led her over to her vehicle. Crouching down in front of her, he took her hands in his, rubbing them between his own. "Better? Do you feel faint?"

"No. I'm okay." Tears streamed down her cheeks. She reached up to wipe them away and soot covered her hand.

"What are you doing here?"

"I saw all the fire trucks and ... I just had a ... I had to come." She covered her face in her hands.

Sam stayed next to her, and when she had stopped crying, he looked into her eyes. "We don't know anything yet. Right?" He moved his head up and down and she followed him.

"Yes, but—"

"No but's. We don't know until we know."

"What happened?"

"We won't know until the fire marshal gives his findings."

"Do you think it was the same person who set the other fires?"

"I couldn't tell you, but I do think this one seems different. Though, why, I couldn't tell you." He looked at her. "I can't leave, but I could get one of the others to drive you home. You shouldn't be here."

The message Sam sought to convey was clear. If they did find Carson's body in the debris, he didn't want her there to see it.

"I can drive myself." Anne sniffed, and Sam handed her a pack of tissues he pulled from one of his many pockets.

"Okay. Let me help you to stand up and then I'll determine if I concur." He helped Anne to her feet and walked her around to the driver's side. He settled her in the seat. "Are you sure? I can easily get someone to drive you."

"Thanks, but no. I really want to be alone." She gripped the steering wheel.

"All right. You'll need to back out and then turn your car. We can't have it closer."

Anne nodded affirmation of his instructions.

Sam moved away from the door and Anne backed up a way down the road. She then slowly made her way down Old Ranch.

A car was barreling toward her. It was a deputy's car. One with a dented front fender. Ruiz.

The deputy's vehicle shot past hers and he cast a quick glance before continuing toward the burning structure.

Ruiz. He has to be El Toro, or he has to know who is. First, Dale killed, and now ... no, no. I refuse to think about.

By the time Anne arrived home, she saw Hope's car in her driveway. Kandi and Hope ran down to the car when they saw her. As she exited the car, the three embraced.

"We just heard. It's all over town."

"I'm, *like*, so, so, sorry." Kandi whimpered.

"Me too, sweetie." Anne caught herself before she broke down again.

Hope took her arm. "Let's get you inside. I'll make you some hawthorn tea."

"Thanks, Hope."

Kandi took Anne's other hand and they walked to the house. Inside, Kandi put a soft blanket around Anne's shoulders. Even though it was the height of summer, the weight and warmth of the blanket comforted Anne.

Once Hope had returned with the tea, the trio sat in silence, sipping the drink. Finally, Anne broke the silence. "What about the Inn? Are we okay over there for now, since we're all here?"

"Don't worry. Stewart said he'd hang out for a while."

Anne took another sip of the warming brew. "How did you all know so fast?"

"Stewart is on the volunteer fire department. They had called them up to be ready in case the fire spread to the forest."

"It had spread to the neighboring area by the trees, but Carson had a large space cleared around his home so I'm sure they've contained it."

Hope reached over and patted Anne's knee. "Don't give up hope yet."

Anne pressed her lips tightly together and nodded. "I'm trying to be optimistic, but you didn't see the house. It was totally engulfed. No one could have survived."

Kandi quipped, "He could have driven into town. You know, *like,* on some errands."

Anne smiled at the encouragement offered by the young woman. "Yes, except his car was there. Ruined too."

Loud banging on the back door startled the women.

"You stay there. I'll get it." Hope set her cup down on the table and went to the back.

When she returned, it was with Mary Smith.

"Is it true?" Mary spat out.

Anne stiffened. "Is *what* true?"

"An officer was killed. Sheriff Carson's house is destroyed."

"Why do you want to know?"

Mary didn't respond. She turned back toward the kitchen and exited the house.

Hope shook her head. "What is going on?"

Anne stood up. "I don't know. But I'm going to find out if it's the last thing I do."

Chapter Thirty

Tragedy filled the next morning's paper with the report of total loss of Carson's house. According to the fire marshal, the fire began in response to a gas explosion. The fire had been so intense that they would have to call in experts to sift through the debris. They weren't reporting on any fatalities. They were asking people to stay away from the area.

Anne had tossed and turned all night with nightmares. She was running, running from something. A bull. Chasing her. But as she tried to get away, flames licked at her heels. She couldn't breathe.

Anne woke up. She opened her eyes to see Mouser laying on her chest. Seeing her open eyes, Mouser touched her cheek and purred. "Oh, Mouser. Sweet boy." She picked him up and laid him down on the bed next to her, but instead of curling up, he bounded off the bed and out of the room.

Tears sprung unbidden. "No. You've got to stop it. This won't help you find out who did this."

Carson's words came to her ears. "ND, stay out of it."

How many times had he told her to leave it to the professionals? That she wasn't a real detective.

"You're right." She screamed out into the void. "I don't know what I'm doing. I've only made things worse. For Hope. Now for you." She sat up and hugged her knees to her chest.

Anne acknowledged that she wasn't a seasoned detective and lacked many of the skills needed to solve complicated crimes, but she couldn't sit by and do nothing. She reviewed everything in her mind. What had Carson said about people doing things they never thought they would? And what about what Bill had told her about a money opportunity? She had no other roads to pursue, so she decided to visit the Connors.

When Anne arrived, a forlorn-looking man greeted her. Bill guided her into the living room area where Lori sat. The woman's face was red from crying. Anne rushed over to her. "I'm so sorry, Lori."

"Thanks." She squeezed Anne's hand.

"Yes." Anne took a chair opposite from Lori. "I've come also because I want to ask you some questions, Bill."

He sighed. "Fine. But how about some mint lemonade first? I have a feeling I know what you're going to ask."

Anne agreed, and they waited in companionable silence until Bill returned with the drinks. He handed one to Anne and one to Lori. He then took a seat on the couch.

"Bill—"

He raised his hand. "Why don't I tell our story?"

"Okay." Anne looked toward Lori who nodded.

He sighed and took a deep breath. "When Lori got ill, we tried the normal things, but she kept getting weaker and weaker. The pain became unrelenting. They gave her these pain-lollipops and Fentanyl patches. It helped for a time, but she was still going downhill.

"I researched treatments and found that patients were responding to herbs. I went to see Hope, and she prescribed astragalus along with some other herbs. But along the way, I saw more and more articles about people being healed by cannabinoid oil. I asked Lori if she'd consider trying it. It helped, and she could even eat again. But it's an expensive product. I found out that Ray Lawrence would buy the buds and I could use the leaves for juicing. So that helped pay for some oil. But it wasn't enough. Ray said if I added more plants, I could make more money and have more leaf material for Lori." He rubbed his hands together.

"I was all in. I said I'd do it. But then I heard he was selling the pot to kids. Kids! I couldn't be a part of that. We struggled enough with doing it medicinally, but I thought he was selling to adults. Even then it went against my beliefs, but..." He looked at Lori. She smiled at him. "She was doing so much better. The pain had become manageable, and she could eat and keep food down."

He put his head in his hands. "Carson knew. He didn't condone it, that's for sure. But he agreed I was legally within my rights to grow the number of plants I had to use for Lori. He didn't know I was selling the buds to Ray. Then things went south. I heard about the Bennett's place. I'd gotten my plants from them. They wanted to help people, but then Ray wanted them to sell him the product. They'd heard about him selling to kids too. They refused." Bill looked up. "You saw what happened there."

Anne spoke, "Do you know who attacked you?"

Bill shook his head. "I think it was some kid Ray had sent over. He came to get product and I wouldn't give it to him. I told him to get out, and he grabbed one of my plant's containers. That's the last I remember."

"He could have killed you."

"I know. I was lucky." Bill touched the area where a small bandage covered the stitches in his scalp. "Then the Bennett's place burned down. And someone killed Ray. I didn't know what to make of that. But it was something the kid said about El Toro."

He got up and paced the room.

"Cal Bennett called me after I got out of the hospital. They'd been threatened, and when the ETB Corporation offered to buy their property, they sold and left. That's when I realized I'd gotten in way over my head. Cal even said I shouldn't trust anyone in law enforcement." He sat back down.

"I hate to admit it, but I wondered if Carson was involved. Yes, he's Lori's cousin but you don't really know anyone totally, do you?"

"I guess so. But he wouldn't burn down his own house."

Lori grasped her throat. "What!"

Anne looked from Lori to Bill. "But you'd been crying. You said, 'no news is good news'."

"I was crying because I found out the cancer's in remission."

"Maybe I'm missing something, but you said thanks when I said I was sorry. I'm confused."

"Oh, I had a friend going through the same thing. She lost her battle this morning." Lori wadded up a tissue in her hand. "Now, what's this about burning down houses?"

"You haven't seen the paper?"

Bill stopped her. "Anne, please. What is it?"

"I hate to be the one to tell you, but Carson's house burned to the ground yesterday. I thought you would have heard."

"We were in Denver, visiting Lori's friend in hospice. We got home very late and we don't get the paper from town. I usually pick one up when I go into town."

Lori moaned. "Poor Carson. How's he doing?"

Anne fought to keep control. "They haven't found him."

"You don't mean—" Lori gasped. "Bill!"

He rushed to her side and held her.

"Nothing's been determined yet. Who knows? He may not have been home."

"His car wasn't there?"

"No. It was." Anne sighed.

"Oh, Bill." Lori buried her face in his shirt and wept.

Anne struggled to remain composed. She stood. "I'm sorry. I have to go." She left before she broke down in front of them.

"I'll walk you out." Bill rose and kissed Lori's hand. "I'll be back in a minute."

Once they were out of earshot, Bill took Anne by the arm. "You think Carson was in the house, don't you?"

Anne struggled to mouth the words. "Yes."

"Poor Carson." He led Anne outside and shut the front door behind him.

"Bill, what do you know of this El Toro?"

"From what I gathered from Cal, it was someone not from the Springs."

"Did he ever say anything about a woman being involved?"

"I overheard Ray talking to someone on the phone one day. It sounded like a woman's voice. Other than that, I don't know."

"How long ago was that?"

"Right before Ray died in the fire."

Anne thought back. Mary hadn't shown up in town until after Ray died. Was that why she had come?

"What about Deputy Ruiz?"

"What about him?" Bill kicked at the gravel on the drive.

"Have you heard of him in any connection about drugs or…?"

"No. I know he was on call when the Bennett's place went up."

Anne pulled her keys from her purse. "He was the first one there?"

"Couldn't tell you."

"Who came up after they attacked you?"

"I think Lori said it was Officer Dale."

"And now he's dead."

Chapter Thirty-One

Anne said goodbye to Bill and left for home. Thoughts swirled in her mind.

Ray Lawrence. Selling drugs to kids. Found dead at the Bennett's.

Bennetts growing marijuana. Greenhouse destroyed. Ray killed.

Deputy Ruiz. Fairly new to town. First on the scene at the Bennetts.

Bennett's place sold. Gate has a bull on it. El Toro.

Ruiz and Mary. Were they working together?

Was Mary the woman? Had she come to the Springs after Ray's death?

Carson overseeing Bennett investigation. Jailed for starting a fire at Hope's.

Officer Dale. First on the scene at Bill's. Dies right before meeting.

Arson materials found at Dale's. Carson cleared. Carson's house destroyed.

Why?

That simple question kept playing over and over in her mind. Why go after Carson? Did he know something?

Anne had no more answers than she'd had before. Something kept alluding her.

Back at her house, she wrote everything out on paper, but nothing appeared or led her further.

Maybe she could talk to Sam. She got back in her car and drove out to Sam's. As she pulled up to the cabin, Hank bounded down the steps toward her. That was a good sign, as Hank often went with Sam unless he was working. It probably meant Sam was home.

Anne walked toward the back deck and heard Sam's voice and a woman's voice. Mary.

She was about to leave when Sam appeared at the top of the stairs. "Anne. Good to see you. Come on up."

Anne took the stairs and saw that Mary was sitting on a lounger on the deck.

"Hello."

"Hi," Mary responded. "I owe you an apology."

"You do?"

"Yes. I shouldn't have come on so forcefully, I behaved badly, and I hope you'll forgive me."

Said the spider to the fly.

"Sure."

"We've come from a hike and were just taking a break before I take Mary back to the Inn. How can I assist you?"

Polite. Formal. So unlike Sam. Anne realized that they really had moved on.

"It's nothing. I wondered—"

"There's no news. I wish I could tell you something more. Trust me. I want to know too."

"Do you at least know what happened?"

"It's like what's being said. Gas leak or something and the house exploded."

"But you would have found... at least... fragments." Anne shot a quick glance over at Mary, who remained stoic in her demeanor.

"Nothing yet. I'm sure we'll hear something today or tomorrow though."

"Okay. Well, I thought I'd stop by for just a minute."

"I'm glad you did."

The more she thought about Sam with Mary, she felt she had to do something.

She turned back to the woman. "How's Deputy Ruiz?"

The woman stared at Anne. "I'm sorry. What do you mean?"

"I've seen you two together quite a bit, I thought maybe you had become friends..." She left it hanging with implied intent.

"I've seen him when he came out here to fish but other than that we only exchange greetings if we see each other. We're not friends." Mary crossed her arms.

"My bad. I guess I misunderstood."

"Yes. You misunderstood. No problem."

Anne felt at a loss. She had gotten no new information. She turned where she could see Mary's reaction but asked Sam, "Have you been out to the new event center? I think it's got a bull on the gate and it's called, um, El Toro or something."

Sam answered but Anne focused on Mary's response. The woman tensed but it was slight and only visible since Anne had been looking for a reaction.

"I'm sorry, what?"

"I said, Stewart's upset and so are lots of other workers as they haven't employed too many locals in the building."

"Yes, I'd heard that too."

Anne furrowed her brow. "Now that you mention it, I wonder why."

Mary rose from the lounger in one quick movement. "I'm sure it's the way that company prefers to work."

"Is it? Do you know the company?" Anne faced the woman.

"No. I'm thinking that's probably the reason." She turned to Sam. "I think I will head back to the Inn. Still on for dinner this evening?"

He smiled at her. "Yes. I'll take you."

"Thanks, but no. I think I'll get in a short run."

A hike and now a run? Was this woman for real?

She turned to Anne. "I'm really enjoying my stay at the Inn. It's been very nice. I can tell that you all have invested a lot into it."

Anne felt a chill. Was the woman threatening her or the Inn?

She waved goodbye and jogged off down the trail.

"Sam?"

"Yes?" He turned to her.

"It's not my place, but I don't think Mary is…"

"Is what?"

"Well, take her name for instance. I mean, come on. Mary Smith. I could pick a better name."

Sam laughed. "Are you kidding me? You're giving me love life advice."

"I'm simply saying, how much do you know about her?"

"Not as much as I'd like." He wiggled his eyebrows.

Anne swatted at him. "Okay. But be it upon your own head. Don't forget that I didn't warn you."

"Warn me against a woman or all women?"

Anne sighed. "Okay, cards on the table. I think she may be involved in a drug cartel. Possibly with Deputy Ruiz."

Sam burst out laughing. "You've got to be kidding me. I have to give it to you—your imagination is something."

"I'm serious, Sam." She crossed her arms.

"Sorry. But there's no way she's involved in something like that. Or Ben either."

"Ben?"

"Ruiz. His name's Benjamin. But he goes by Ben."

"He hasn't been here that long, and Mary only showed up after someone killed Ray."

"Those are facts. But I can't see either of them being involved in anything like that."

"Maybe that's because they want you to think that."

His cell phone rang. He held up a finger. "Powers speaking." He listened. "Yes. Yes. Okay. Thanks for calling." He clicked the phone off.

"That was the head of the crime scene technicians. No human remains found."

Anne grabbed Sam in a hug, laughing and crying.

Carson was alive.

But if he was alive, where was he?

Chapter Thirty-Two

"That's a good question," Hope responded when Anne gave her the news. "It doesn't seem like him to not let people know what's going on, but I guess I really don't know him that well."

They were sitting in the Inn's kitchen where Kandi was making a batch of chocolate chip cookies to put in the guest's rooms.

Anne took a swipe of the rich dough before Kandi pulled the dough away. "Now, stop that. If you eat all the dough, I won't have enough for the actual cookies." She moved over toward the kitchen counter.

"He has been going up to Denver quite a bit lately. Maybe he went up there and he forgot to turn off the gas on his stove or something."

Hope twisted her mouth. "I can't see him being forgetful like that, and he would have come home at night and seen the house."

"I guess." Anne sighed loudly. "Oh, have you seen Mary Smith? She was out at Sam's."

Kandi shook her head. "Nope. Of course, I've been back here much of the morning. She's usually out early in the morning and often has a continental breakfast versus dining with the other guests." She pulled out the cooking tray. "She's kind of, *like,* a loner. I've tried talking to her, and she's polite, but she doesn't say much."

"Yes, she is that." Anne faced Hope. "Do you think she's involved with the drugs situation?"

"I couldn't say. Maybe it's another woman."

"It could be. But who?"

"Maybe it's, *like,* Thelma at the police station." Kandi giggled.

"I don't see her being on the wrong side of the law. I can see her bashing some criminal over the head with her big black purse." Anne widened her hands. "What does she even keep in that thing?"

Hope chuckled. "I believe she's a knitter."

"Ah, okay. Then that makes sense. Hmmmm."

"What is it, Anne?"

"Kandi actually might have something with what she said."

Hope moved over so Kandi could set the trays on the sturdy wooden table. "You can't seriously think Miss Thelma could be part of a gang?"

"Oh, no. But it could be someone we're not even considering."

Kandi scooped out the dough onto the baking sheets.

"Like who?"

"I don't know."

Stewart came in and the women all responded with hearty greetings.

"I stopped by to see if you'd heard anything about Carson."

Anne filled him in on the latest and asked if he had any idea where Carson might be.

"Sorry, no. But this has got to be the strangest time around here."

"Why do you say that?"

"Oh, do you know Gary Neal?"

"No," they all chimed.

"He's our local building inspector. He won some kind of contest and he got an all-expense paid trip to Alaska. He doesn't even remember entering anything, but it's been a dream he's had forever. He and his wife left a few days ago."

"Did you say building inspector?"

Stewart twisted a chair around and straddled it. "Yeah, why?"

"Is he the inspector for the Bennett place?"

"Yes. He is over the entire department. Why?"

"Nothing." Anne stood up. "Unless I'm needed any more over here, I'm going home. I didn't sleep well last night, and I might take a nap."

"You're so, *like,* old." Kandi winked at Anne.

"Ha. Wait until you get older. You'll realize that naps are a luxury and have great benefits," Anne retorted.

At home, Anne set to work. She could take a nap, but she knew one thing for sure. She needed to get a closer look at the Bennett place. She knew from Stewart that most of the workers had moved off the property and only a few were still on site. Of those, they went home on the weekends. If she followed the route she and Carson took, she could enter the grounds that way.

That night, she tossed and turned and was up at five. She grabbed her backpack which held a flashlight and cutters, along with her phone, water, and snacks. She'd dressed in browns and greens, hoping that would give her more cover.

Anne walked out to the trailhead at the back of the property when she sensed something. She turned around and saw Mary Smith in the shadows of the gazebo.

"Oh, Mary. You startled me." Anne held her hand up to her chest.

Mary finished tying her shoe. "Going somewhere?"

Anne fumbled for an answer. "Birdwatching."

"Oh yes, you said you were into that. Early isn't it?"

"That's when you have to go. You can catch them at the crack of dawn." Anne motioned to her. "You going running?"

"Yes. I like to get my ten miles in early."

Ten Miles. Yikes.

"Well, if you ever see me running, you better too, because the only reason I'd run is that a bear was chasing me."

"I thought you shouldn't run from wild animals." Mary adjusted the balaclava on her head.

"You shouldn't. It's a joke."

"Oh. Funny." She didn't laugh.

"Which way are you headed?" Anne couldn't have this woman see where she was going.

"I figured I'd go out to Sam's. Then if he's up, I'll see if I can entice him to take me to Donna's Donuts."

"Donuts? You? I would have thought you were one of those anti-sugar people." Anne smiled at the woman as they both walked to the trail.

Mary laughed. "I know about balance. That's why I run. Then if I eat something unhealthy, it doesn't end up on my hips." She pulled one leg up behind her in a hamstring stretch, then followed with the other.

Anne wanted to retort that the woman had no body fat to speak of, but she needed to get going. She had to end the conversation. "Well, have a good run."

She waved at the woman who smiled and said, "Have a good time spying."

Mary set off at a slow warm-up pace. As soon as the woman rounded the bend and was no longer in sight, Anne decided she'd jog to do some catching up on time. She'd gotten a quarter of a mile, when she slowed to a walk. Huffing, she wondered, who does that for fun?

A noise sounded behind her. She swiftly turned but saw nothing. Even though she knew animals lived in the forest, she didn't want to meet one on the trail. She picked up her pace.

As she neared the spot where Carson had taken her off the trail, she turned back behind her. She stared into the forest but could see nothing, but she didn't feel alone. Was a mountain lion tracking her?

Fear at being stalked made her shiver. She took out the flashlight from her bag. It was a heavy item, and she'd almost chosen to leave it at home but now she was glad to have it. If nothing else, she could use it as a weapon.

Searching the area from the spot they'd left the trail, Anne noticed some broken branches. She walked over to it. Sure enough, someone had constructed a simple cairn under the cover of scrub oak. Had Carson done that? Or someone else?

She turned back once more and saw nothing on the trail. She began her climb to the upper ridge. It took longer than she remembered with Carson. Maybe because she kept turning at any snap of a branch.

Quit being so silly. Animals live here, and it doesn't mean it's a bear or mountain lion out to get you.

As she neared the edge, she got down and pulled the binoculars from her pack. She also pulled out an old broken weaved hat. Last night she'd painted it brown and green. She sat down and stuck grasses and dead leaves to it.

Ha! It pays to watch those old shows on staying camouflaged. She put the hat on and secured it with the cord. She grabbed the binoculars.

Cautiously, she raised her head over the ridge to look down on the Bennett's old homestead. The trailers were now gone and the shells of two homes were off away from the house. Anne scanned the area. No signs of anyone. She looked toward the front gate. It was closed. She couldn't see any vehicles.

Anne inched closer to the edge and swung the binoculars over to the largest structure—the event center. On the side she spied a door with a window in it. It wouldn't hurt to go look and see inside.

Anne pulled the backpack over to her. She took off the hat and put the binoculars' strap around her neck. She popped on a cap. If anyone stopped her, she'd give them the same story about birdwatching. She unstrapped a retractable walking stick from the bag to help on her descent. Gingerly, she descended the hill, crossing back and forth, stopping behind trees to see if she could detect any movement. It took a long time to make it to the edge of the property. To keep up the appearance of being a birdwatcher, she stepped out into the clearing and looked up into the bank of trees off to her left.

No one called out to her. That was a good sign.

Anne continued to stay close to the trees until she got within yards of the event center. She picked up the binoculars and scanned the trees again then turned them toward the house. No vehicle. No movement.

Anne let out her breath. She wanted to run over to the event center but forced herself to meander and look up into the trees. She didn't like being this exposed, but what else could she do? As she walked along the event center, she continued to scan for any movement on the grounds. Then she was at the door. She took one last glance behind her, then cupped her hands over her eyes to see in the door.

As her eyes adjusted to the darker interior, she saw that this part of the hall was small.

She stifled a scream. Someone was looking at her. Wait. No. She squinted at the reflection. They had mirrored all the walls making the room to appear much larger than it was. In the far corner of the room, another door led to the other part of the center.

She tried the door. Locked. She looked into the room again. Boxes were stacked in the middle and what looked like a pile of carpet. It moved.

Carson!

Anne jiggled the door handle. Pulling the binoculars from around her neck, she smashed the window. Carefully, Anne removed the glass until she could get her hand inside and unlock the door.

She ran across the room. "Carson! Carson!"

He moaned. As she reached him, she could see his hands and ankles were tied. His eyes fixed on hers.

He struggled to get the words out. "Drugged. Go."

"I will not leave you."

A male voice answered. "You're right there."

Anne jumped up from where she'd been bending down next to Carson. The man remained in the shadows, but she could see his bearded face and shoulder-length hair. Sunglasses hid his eyes.

Was this El Toro?

She stepped closer to Carson and her eyes searched the area. No one else.

A crunch of glass. Anne swiveled to see Mary Smith.

"Hola." She rattled off something in Spanish that Anne didn't understand.

So Mary was in on the drugs.

The man lowered his arm, and it was the first time Anne realized he carried a gun.

Mary switched to English. "It seems that we have a problem."

"No problema. I've got it under control."

Something nagged at Anne. The man's voice. Where had she heard it before?

Carson had righted himself to a sitting position. Anne turned back to help him.

"Don't move." The man raised his gun.

From the corner of her eye, Anne watched as Mary launched herself toward the man. In mere seconds, the man was on the ground, Mary's foot was on his back and his arm was twisted up behind him. She watched as the woman spoke into her watch. "Situation contained. Approach."

From the various doors, men dressed in swat gear advanced.

Mary hauled the man up.

"What? Who?" Anne struggled to say the words. Then her mouth dropped as she realized whose voice it was.

"Chief Everett?"

Mary waited until the man was cuffed and then pulled the hat from his head. A wig attached to the hat came with it. The beard must be a fake too.

"But…" She turned back to Carson, who stood next to her. "Carson… what?"

"Take him away," Mary said.

After the men had exited the room, Deputy Ruiz came inside.

"You got him, Deputy. You too, Sheriff. Good work."

Anne turned to Carson. "You have a lot of explaining to do."

"Fine. Later." He slumped against her.

Chapter Thirty-Three

Carson spent a day in the hospital getting checked out. The following day, Anne picked him up and took him to her house. She now sat on the couch next to Carson. Across from them sat Mary Smith. Deputy Ruiz had also joined the group.

Carson began, "I kept thinking that we were missing something." He turned to Anne. "You gave me an idea when you kept talking about El Toro. The Bull."

"What was it?"

"E.T.B." He responded. "That's the name of the corporation for the Bennett event center. I'd been writing some things down on paper and I held it up to look at it. That's when it hit me. I took it over to a mirror and I saw it."

"Saw what?"

Carson flipped his hand. "A mirror turns it around. And there it was. B.T.E."

"Huh?"

"El Toro. The Bull. Bradley Thomas Everett."

Mary took up the story. "We've—"

"We?" Anne inquired.

"DEA," Mary responded. "We've been after this group for a while. We were tipped off by Deputy Ruiz.

After the fire at the Bennetts, we had to get someone on site. Someone had found out that Ray Lawrence was playing both sides of the fence."

Anne gasped. "He was an informant?"

"Yes. We kept getting all these little fish, but we needed the brains behind the operation. He was really smart to use foster kids that were set to be out of the system. There would be no questions when they took off. With Carolan Springs out of the way, it would be easy to up production and transport it out on I-70. We caught up with Lawrence and, let's say, we made him a deal he couldn't refuse."

"I guess I'm not up on things. It wouldn't seem that growing pot—"

Mary clasped her hands together. "It wasn't just pot. Everett was having it laced with other drugs. He wanted to get people hooked on the product and then he had them under his thumb. He could make them do anything at that point."

"Oh my gosh."

Carson replied, "Officer Dale figured out that Everett was involved. When Everett heard him talking to you, he knew he had to shut him up. When we were at the scene, Everett said that the cell phone service was bad. That stuck in my mind. Because how could Dale have texted you to come later? And why would he have picked that time to end it? It didn't make sense.

"When we got there, he said that Dale had driven off the road. That he was dead. What probably happened was that Dale was unconscious when he was driven up the mountain. Then Everett put him behind the wheel and let it go off the cliff."

Anne stopped him. "But he could have gone off the cliff accidently."

"True. But that's where Everett messed up. He had gone down to set up the scene as a suicide. At that point, Dale was still alive. Gravely hurt, but alive." He sat back on the couch. "He hurried back up the hill and waited for us. He told us Dale was dead and we accepted it. As soon as we left, he hurried back down and finished Dale off."

"Are you saying he shot him? We would have heard something."

"I wondered about that too. I also wondered how he'd got the car off the road."

Deputy Ruiz took up the story. "While you and Carson were away, I had to figure who was behind it. I had to stay clear of Carson because he could have been in on it too." He spoke to Carson. "Sorry. No offense."

"None taken. You were doing your job and that means you were unbiased in your methods. That's the sign of competent lawman."

Ruiz grinned. "Thanks. Anyway, when Hope's shop got torched, it seemed too perfect. A set-up. With Carson out of the way, that meant that the police would handle the case out at the Bennetts. It was too convenient."

"Agree. That's what I thought." Carson replied. "Dale's death kept nagging at me. I took a dirt bike and rode up to the site."

"Wouldn't the crime scene technicians have gone over the site?" Anne turned toward him.

"Yes." Carson nodded. "But I believe that Everett set the site up the way he wanted it perceived. Of course, if his DNA showed up, it wouldn't be an issue as he'd been the first on the scene. That was the first question. How did he know where to look for Dale?"

"Then what happened?" Anne motioned for him to continue.

"I borrowed a very important tool and took the motorcycle up there."

Anne crossed her legs. "What was that?"

"A metal detector. I stood where the car was at the window. I mapped out how far I could throw a rock and started hunting in that area. Sure enough, I found a silencer. Everett knew it would be buried under the leaves and it would be better to not have it on him in case they collected his clothing."

Carson sighed before continuing. "I was on my way home when Ruiz let me know about my house. Everett must have realized I'd be on to him. I'd set the house up to seem like I'd be back shortly. He must have set some trigger to cause the explosion."

"Do you know how worried we all were?"

"Yes. I was going to come over and let you know but I needed a bit more time to be able to come out to the Bennett place and look around. Everett would think I'd been killed, and I needed to use that time before they shared that no body had been found. Unfortunately, he saw me at the Bennetts. He was dressed up as a worker, so by the time I realized it was him, well, I don't remember anything after that until I woke up and knew I'd been drugged."

Anne turned toward Mary. "All this time you were trying to get Everett?"

"We didn't know it was Everett until recently. We did know there was some connection with the Bennett place. We also knew that the building inspector was probably about to have an accident. Luckily, he got an all-expense paid trip to Alaska."

Anne laughed. "I wondered how that had happened."

"Yes, it will be good because when he comes back, he's going to have to explain the large deposit he received in his bank account."

"Is the Bennett place structurally un-sound?"

"Oh, no. It's a front. The back of the event center was to be a large grow operation. Recently it was learned that a large insurance policy had been taken out on the place. We figured Everett felt things were getting too close to home, so he'd burn it down, collect the insurance money and get rid of Carson in one go."

Carson squeezed her hand. "You saved me, ND."

"I did?"

Mary answered, "I followed you out to the Bennetts. When I saw you go in, I called in Ruiz and back-up. Carson's right. We needed proof, and you gave it to us."

"But what about Officer Dale? He should have his name cleared and justice."

Ruiz stood up. "We got word that Dale had left all his suspicions and evidence he'd gathered in a safety deposit box. His lawyer had been out of town and only came back recently. He turned it over to the DA's office. I think there's enough evidence that Everett will go away for a long time."

"I'm happy to hear that." Anne rose as Mary stood to leave. "Does this mean goodbye?"

"I'm not sure. I've come to enjoy this little town." Mary smiled.

Anne quipped, "I would have at least thought that you would have picked a better undercover name than Mary Smith."

The woman threw back her head and laughed. "That's my real name. You can't beat it for undercover assignments."

After saying their goodbyes, Anne sat on the couch with Carson.

"What now?"

He shrugged. "I don't know. Take some time off, I think."

His phone rang. "Carson." Anne watched as he listened.

He frowned.

"What is it?"

"That time off will have to wait. Everett escaped."

"Where could he have gone?" Anne watched as Carson prepared to leave.

"I don't know. He knows there will be an APB out on him, so he'd need to have a place to hide until he can get out of town."

"Will you let me know if you find out anything?"

He smiled down at her, placing his hands on her arms.

She rolled her eyes. "I get it. But please, be careful."

"I will." He took her hands and kissed each one.

After Carson had left, Anne walked over to the Brandywine Inn. Kandi was chopping up veggies for a crudité tray while Hope hunched over paperwork. Hope looked up as Anne entered. "Hey, lady. I thought you were taking off today."

"I wanted to come over and check in with you all. Everett escaped custody."

Kandi set down the knife. "Oh no. How?"

"Good question. I figure he must have known his capture was a possibility, so he had someone ready to help him. It happened as the van was leaving the Springs." Anne sat down and grabbed a carrot stick.

"Wow. That's crazy."

"Yes. No telling where he is or how desperate he'll become if he's found."

"I wonder if it was that woman." Kandi picked up peppers draining on the sink.

Anne swung around to Kandi. "I'd forgotten all about that. We—or at least, I had always thought the woman was Mary. But since it wasn't, who is it?"

Kandi cut a piece of pepper and pointed it at Anne. "I told ya, Thelma." She laughed and then took a bite of the pepper.

"Oh, my gosh. Of course. Kandi, you're so right."

Kandi bobbed her head. "Huh? I really don't think Thelma…"

"No. Not Thelma. I remember when you said it the first time—we had said something about it being someone you'd never suspect."

Hope raised her hands in mock protest. "I swear. I didn't do it." She grinned.

"Ha Ha. But think about it. Who is the one person who's connected to all this?" She ticked statements off with her fingers. "Ray, pot, teens…"

Kandi's mouth dropped open. "Whoa."

"Yes, whoa."

"I guess I'm missing something." Hope looked from one to the other. "Who?"

"Mrs. Lawrence!" Anne and Kandi squealed at the same time.

Hope covered her mouth, now open in surprise.

Anne grabbed her phone and called Carson. "I know who helped Everett. Mrs. Lawrence." She put the phone on speaker.

Carson's voice came over the cell. "That actually makes sense. I should have heeded what Spencer said."

"What Spencer said?"

"Yes. Don't you remember? He said she was just in it for the money. If she could tell Everett who the bad seeds were, he could easily get them to work for him."

"But I thought no one knew who he was?"

"That was the beauty of it. He could go through so many channels that no one ever knew it was him. He also used Dale to give some of the kids grief. Dale probably never knew he was being used to present a message that even the police were in on it."

"What now?" Anne hunched over the phone.

"I'll get people over to Lawrence's house. Hopefully, we can catch him and put an end to this quickly before anyone else gets hurt."

"Okay. Well, bye."

"Good work, ND." He canceled the call.

Anne looked to see Kandi and Hope grinning from ear to ear. "What?"

Unfortunately, by the time that the police made it to Mrs. Lawrence's, Everett was not there. They did search the house and found enough evidence and testimony from some kids to arrest Mrs. Lawrence.

"What will happen to the kids there?" Anne asked Carson once he'd returned to the Inn.

"I guess they'll go to another foster placement in Denver. Carolan Springs is too small for them here."

Anne rubbed her hands together. "But what about Spencer? He's never going to leave Bear."

"I've thought of that. I even wondered if they would let him stay in my care, but with my house gone, I don't have the means." He shook his head. "I really like the kid, but my hands are tied."

"What if he could stay with me?" Anne pushed her hair off her face.

"You'd do that?"

Anne nodded. "That kid's grown on me and I can't stand the idea of him being taken away from us."

"I agree. He's a good kid. Just had some bad things in the past. He's turned himself around. Let me see what I can do." Carson reached over and grasped Anne's hand. "Are you sure about this? Taking on a teenager, much less a hormonal male, is a job in itself."

"As long as you promise to help me."

"I do."

"Then it's settled. See what I need to do to get temporary custody until all the paperwork gets straightened out."

"You know I love you." He gazed down at her.

"I love you too." Anne was surprised at how quickly she'd responded.

"Ahh, that's, *like*, so sweet." Kandi clapped her hands in delight.

"When did you come in, you little sneak?"

"Just now. I'm so happy. I didn't want to see Spencer leave." She rushed up and caught Anne in a hug. "Now I'll have another brother."

Anne shrugged out of her grasp. "Now hold on there, I never said—"

"Whatever." Kandi winked.

Chapter Thirty-Four

A while later, Spencer arrived carrying all his belongings in a black plastic trash-bag. Anne showed him to a room at the end of the hallway that had an adjoining bathroom.

"Make yourself at home, Spence. Let me know if there's anything else you need."

He nodded, but Anne's heart hurt at the forlorn look on his face.

Kandi came over soon after and invited Spencer to go with her and Stewart to see a new superhero movie at the local theater. After he'd left, Carson came over and said there was no sign of Everett. They didn't think he'd made it out of town, but the searches were coming up empty.

"I think I know where he is."

"Okay, why don't you let me in on it, ND?"

"Bill and Lori's."

Carson motioned for her to continue. "What makes you say that?"

"Think about it. It's out of the way. He knows Bill will do whatever he says if he threatens to harm Lori."

"Certainly a thought."

Anne grabbed her keys. "Come on. Let's go."

"Not so fast there. If he is there, we don't want Lori or Bill to get hurt. Or even Everett for that matter."

"Look. At this point, it's just a hunch. How about we go and scope out the place?"

Carson stood still, and Anne waited as he thought through her suggestion. "Let me bring Ruiz into the loop first." He unhooked the phone from his belt and talked into it. When done, he said, "Let's go."

Anne could feel the tension as the pair drove out to the Connor's property. As they came up the long drive, Carson kept looking left and right. Anne pulled up into the driveway and parked the car.

"I need you to do what I say when I say. Deal?" He looked pointedly at her.

"Deal."

They got out of the car and walked to the front door. Bill opened it. His demeanor let them know something was off. "Hey, you two. I wish you would have called. Lori's not feeling too well right now. Maybe you should come back at another time."

"No worries." Carson clapped his hand on Bill's shoulder. "We're here to see you, buddy."

"Well, I…"

"Aren't you going to invite us in Bill?" Anne smiled sweetly.

"Um. Sure. Come in," he said loudly.

They followed him to the back living area where Lori sat in her usual chair. The air was fragrant with the scent of lemongrass.

"Yikes. That's a lot of lemongrass oil. Though I love it," Anne quipped.

"Yes. I spilled some." Lori answered.

"I'm sorry to hear you're not feeling well." Anne moved over to the chair placed next to Lori.

Lori started. "Do you mind? Would you sit on the sofa?"

Strange request. "Um. Sure." Anne moved to the sofa.

"Sorry, but I've been ill and so I'm trying to avoid people as much as possible to keep my immunity up, so I'm keeping space around me."

"Yes, Bill said you weren't feeling well."

Lori looked at Bill and Anne caught a quick glimpse of fear. Did Carson see it too? If he did, he hid it as he sat down next to Anne and pulled her up next to him.

What the…?

"We wanted to stop by and let you know Everett escaped from custody."

"Oh, that's too bad. Isn't it Bill?"

Bill shook his head. "Yes. Too bad."

Carson's voice changed though he kept his posture with his arm around Anne. "Look here. Neither of you even knew he was in custody, am I right? You didn't even ask what he was in custody for, so that leads me to believe you're hiding something."

Lori's voice caught with a sob while Bill remained standing without speaking.

"Now I believe you know where Everett is. I think he's watching us right now. If I'm right, smile and nod your head."

Bill smiled and nodded.

Anne gasped and before she could turn to the window, Carson had brought her over into a kiss. He whispered, "Don't look outside. Keep your focus in here. Smile and laugh."

She did, but she hoped that the shaking she was doing wasn't visible from outside.

Carson smiled again and turned toward Lori. "Lori, can you move from your chair? If you can't, nod yes."

Lori nodded yes.

Oh no. That meant that Everett must have her in his sights. Carson was right. Bill would do anything to ensure Lori was safe.

Carson turned to Bill. "I gather that Everett is in your greenhouse. And he has the gun you just bought."

Bill blinked but said nothing.

"Oh, my gosh." Anne burst out laughing.

Carson started and turned to her. "What's so funny?"

"Lemongrass."

"What?"

"I smelled it when I came in. Bees love it. Right, Bill?"

"Yes."

"I may have accidentally on purpose spilled lemongrass oil on Everett." Lori shrugged.

"Why would you do that?"

"The bees have been swarming. There's a swarm in the greenhouse right now. Bill is going to grab them and put in a box to start a nuc."

"A nuc?"

"It's short for nucleus. Basically, the beginning of another hive. I figured if he was okay with threatening us, then he deserved whatever he got. I know that bees are most docile when swarming but I figured there was always hope he might swat at them and then—watch out."

A scream punctured the air. They all turned to see Everett running out of the greenhouse. He was swatting at bees who were following him.

"Some people get what they deserve," Bill said as he ran over and pulled Lori away from the window. "Come on honey, let's get you out of here."

Once Carson cornered Everett, Bill used smoke and a box with the queen in it to draw the bees away. After being injected with an EpiPen Bill kept at the house, Everett was transferred to the hospital. He wouldn't be escaping this time.

Back at Anne's house, Stewart, Kandi, and Spencer sat around the dining table drinking tea and playing cards. Kandi jumped up and hugged Anne. "Well?"

"They got him."

"We got him," Carson added.

"Good riddance to, *like,* bad garbage."

"It's rubbish." Anne sat down, exhaustion overtaking her.

"Like I said. Garbage, rubbish, trash." Kandi grinned.

Anne shook her head.

"Want to go sit out on the front swing?"

"Sure." She followed Carson outside, covering a yawn with her mouth. The day's events had caught up to her.

They rocked back and forth on the swing. It's movement lulled Anne and she grew drowsy with its lullaby.

Carson spoke quietly, "You know, I've been thinking. Spencer's going to need a male influence. Probably on a regular basis would be my guess. He needs someone that's there consistently. Today, with all that talk about bees and honey, it made me think that maybe planning a honeymoon would be something to think about. What do you say?"

He turned and faced Anne who was sound asleep on his shoulder.

He smiled. "Well, that wasn't the proper way to ask you to marry me anyway." He kissed the top of her head and hugged Anne to his side.

From the Author

I hope you enjoyed reading Honey Homicide, the third book in the backyard farming mystery series. I've come to love the residents of Carolan Springs, and I hope that you have too. If you want to learn more about the residents of Carolan Springs, find out about new releases in this series and others, and be able to partake in fun giveaways then go to www.vikkiwalton.com and sign up to receive my newsletter.

You can also connect with me at: www.facebook.com/vikkiwaltonauthor. I also have a suburban homesteading Facebook page: www.havenesteader.com. I'd love to hear from you. You can contact me directly at vikki@vikkiwalton.com.

Like Anne, I used to be afraid of bees but now as a beekeeper I have learned more about them and understand their importance in our environment. Plus, they make the most wonderful honey! I hope that you'll consider taking a class to learn more about bees, consider becoming a bee guardian through keeping bees, fostering a hive or planting lots of great bee and pollinator friendly plants.

I want to acknowledge my daughter, Jori, who helped me in getting things completed for the book's cover and interior. Her technical experience, along with her artistic talent, is greatly appreciated. I'd also like to think Crystal of Anima Editing for helping provide me that extra set of eyes that all authors require. Her red pen is appreciated. Should you find any errors, they are all mine. Like any author, many others help me along my writing journey and while their names are not listed here, they are greatly appreciated, as are you my dear reader. Thank you for taking your precious time and spending it with the residents of Carolan Springs.

Finally, I hope that if you enjoyed this story you will share it with your friends and on social media as well supply a review.

Thank you.

Thank you for buying this book. You Rock!

To receive special offers, new releases, bonus content, fun giveaways, along with news about latest books or coming series.

Sign up here for my newsletter:
https://vikkiwalton.activehosted.com/f/6

Or visit my website at:
https://www.vikkiwalton.com/

What's Next for Vikki Walton?

Vikki is working on a fun new mystery series set in Comfort, Texas.

Coming Summer 2019!

55625408R00131

Made in the USA
Columbia, SC
16 April 2019